HOW I MAKE MY BED IN HELL

BY KEEGAN NAIDOO

Copyright Page

This is a work of fiction. Names, characters, places, and incidents are products of the author's imagination, and are used fictitiously. Any resemblance to actual persons, living or dead, events, or locales is entirely coincidental.

Title: How I Make My Bed in Hell

ISBN: 978-0-620-92862-5(print)
ISBN: 978-0-620-92863-2(e-book)
ISBN: 978-0-620-92864-9(audio)

Acknowledgement

There was a time when I was questioning myself if I am nothing as a person? Like most people, I also have ups and downs in my life. I did a lot of good and bad things to others. The world's reality also hit me so hard to the point that I once lost my way back into my life. I thought, at some point in my life, that I'd be gone forever. I never felt valued enough on this earth, but God has always been good to me. I would love to give my appreciation to Him for showing me the light once again in my darkest moments. God made a way for me to meet my wife.

For my wife, I want to thank you for helping me make my dream come true. Thank you for the patience in listening and reading my story for a decade. I've been keeping my fictional tale for so many years, and you made it happen; you help me bring this book out. I appreciate my in-laws for giving me your hand, and trusting me that I will love you forever until my last day.

I would also like to thank mum and dad for raising a man like me. I might be a pain in the neck for both of you most of the time, but God knows that I honour you. To my nieces, I am so proud to see both of you fulfilling your dreams, and enjoying yourselves in this time.

Thank you to all the people who believe in me, and I am still grateful to those who never believe me; it actually made a difference in my perspective.

Lastly, I would like to dedicate my artwork to my son Pablo. You are small enough to read this, my child, but I hope that, one day, when you read my book, you'll be proud of me, and it will inspire you to reach the moon and enjoy the stars in your journey, while getting into a beautiful future waiting for you.

Table of Contents

Chapter 1: The Holiday

Have you ever seen a creature that gives a feeling of lingering disturbance? Have you ever witnessed someone moving themselves to go inside thoroughly to fulfil their licentious desire? The reminiscence is incomparably crystal clear, the nights of forcing and the days of a nightmare. A faceless monster, obscuring under our bed, is choosing between us. He is not frightened to get caught, and he is not horrified knowing the repercussion of his act. The faceless monster was lurking in the shadows under my bed every night, concealing himself and waiting for his supper. He has been hiding for years, but it seemed that I'm the only one who could surprisingly see him, or maybe not.

Until I stopped.

I stopped staring under the bed, believing that I am too young to understand the occurrence of something, and I cannot perceive the polarity of real-life and illusion. The sun shines in the morning, and the moon blooms at night.

I sleep mumbling to myself that everything is a dream; from the cry, the moan, and the groan, all are just parts of a nightmare. It is not the actuality; it is a horrifying dream. I rise and shine just like a sun, knowing that the monster is still hiding. There's a hunch inside of me that the faceless monster unceasingly belies himself. I know that he is still there waiting for his prey. However, I did not look back. I never did.

I chose not to look again because no one is going to believe me; I am just a little boy running around and playing blamelessly. I continue in life and annihilate all the illusion I've been keeping. I carry on playing as if nothing happened.

There is no faceless monster. I don't have to be terrified; there is no cry nor groan.

■■

"Lovely introduction and nice line," I whispered while reading the book that presents itself to me. It is smeared with dirt, the pages are already tearing apart, and it doesn't have a pleasant cover; in fact, I don't even know how I got this book.

"I think I'll give this a try," I told myself, and I continue reading.

"People want their dreams to come true, but they didn't know that night terror is a dream too."

It was a frosty month of December of year 1965, the snowdrifts scattered and covered the whole place outside. The chill of the wind kissed my cheeks and wanted to embrace me, but the warmth of my fur kept me moving. However, I could still feel the cold inside my bone. I was sitting outside waiting for our relatives to come and stay with us. It's been a year or two since I last saw them. The excitement made me numb that I literally waited for an hour for them to come. I just can't wait to play.

And then they came.

Aunt Lorette and Uncle Paul, mum's brother, came with their two sons. They are Willy and Garry. Mervin also came with his sister Addie, but unfortunately, their parents were working in Australia and couldn't make it to visit. Diana was also there; she's all by herself. Diana lost her sister and mum when she was young. She didn't have anyone anymore. Auntie Lorette and Uncle Paul took the responsibility to look after her 'til now.

It was filled with happiness, and the laughter was overflowing. My older brother Anthony and I hugged each one of them and gave them a welcoming kiss. Auntie Lorette is average looking, while uncle Paul has a solid Latin look: brownish skin, masculine body, and very dark hair. Other than that, I discerned that my cousins grew a little bit. I am not talking about their appearance though, but how they behaved and how they spoke. They looked more well-mannered than me. I think it is me who didn't mature yet. I'm like a seed planted into the soil that badly needs to sprout so someone can see what and who am I.

I am not just a little boy; I am more than that.

Thereafter, our mum made a cottage pie as a main dish, and a lovely fruit salad for dessert. We were at a long table, eating the mouth-watery food. They were all talking about their long day and gave compliments to each other. My Uncle Paul and Auntie Lorette were continuously showing praises towards Anthony. Well, everyone can see that he is an incredibly well-mannered, soft-spoken child. My mom is so proud of Anthony although he is adopted; it is no secret to everyone but never spoken about. He would constantly groom her hair, and assist her with housework; he can cook, clean and do domestic chores.

Anthony is the kind of son that every parent will definitely pray for. His angelic eyes and sweet adorable smile can make everyone's heart pound. His dazzling brown eyes complement his soft and supple brunette hair with his warm skin tone. I wish I had them too. Who wouldn't be proud to have a lovely child?

After the meal, we decided to sit and speak for a while, 'til our parents told us that they would visit some friends. They assured us that they'll be back before midnight and assigned my brother to take charge of taking care of us. We didn't do anything aside from appreciating the excellent time. The loneliness that I felt instantly disappeared; it's been a long time since I enjoyed and spent time with them. We were so many kids inside the house. I can still remember how rowdy we were. Some of us started to horseplay, while the rest were our audiences, laughing and cheering us on all of the mess and misbehaving that we did. Such a fantastic day indeed.

However, it wasn't always a good time.

There's always a time when they were making fun of me because I was a bit slow, mentally and physically, running around, smashing people with my plump body. I'm just a kid; all I know is observing, watching, and playing—a complete opposite of my brother.

We were blessed and cursed, at the same time, to have cousins born in the same year as ours, and be compared with the other siblings. Nonetheless, I can say that not for a moment that it bothered me. Not at all.

■■■

It was half-past eleven in the evening, and all decided to sleep. I went to my room within an ace of doze.

Time past by, and I sensed a horripilation on my body. I slowly opened my eyes, but there's something inside me saying that I have to keep my eyes closed. But I couldn't. I think I was dreaming. I heard someone crying. The despair and fear of silence were swallowing the corners inside. The moan, and the dead noise after that, gave me cold shivers. I was horrified; that fear inside me went to my blood, and ran down through my veins. I wanted to scream, but I don't know if it was an illusion, or the monster came back.

"He is not true. But who is crying? Who is moaning?" I was asking myself while lying down in the middle of nowhere.

■■

I woke up in the morning, and saw the inviting food that our parents made. Sadly, luck was not on my destiny. The three older cousins, my brother, Willy, and Diana, left our heels cold. We cannot sit and eat with them. They woke up early, and were already in the middle of ingesting their food, so they have to finish it first. It is a gesture of respect not to bother them. I saw my brother alongside Willy gobbling up, enjoying their food, talking and laughing, unlike Diana. She's not talking much and looked like she had a stormy night, just like me.

Diana is always pretty; in every angle, she's always stunning. The circle face of hers, with pink lips which perfectly fit her long brown beach wave hair, or maybe I was too young, so everyone for me is good-looking.

I don't know, and I'm really not sure.

One thing that I'm sure about is she's out of herself right now. She's not like this; she was a bubbly and very cheerful girl despite her painful life. But only God knows.

Yeah, I think only God knows.

The wait was over; they cleaned the table and walked away from the place. My mum placed more food for the younger cousins: I, Mervin, Garry, and Addie.

The aroma that vapoured on the coffee woke my embodiment. The bacon that was cooked ideally was so easy to bite in my mouth. The heated butter that made the crusty bread soft was just the best combination to complete my morning.

Then Garry unfolded a conversation.

I looked at him, appalled; he's asking each one of us if we heard noises and emulating everything that seemed to be so funny, but every one of us was stunned. Mervin and Addie denied, as well as me. We all continued to eat. Meanwhile, I couldn't talk. I got frightened thinking that the monster making noise under the bed and the shadow were not a nightmare,

"What if it's true?" I asked.

He became more descriptive. He imitated the sound. The essence of the place became excruciating for me. I could not complete my food. I wanted to stand up. But apparently, I felt the gravity pulling my body; it was just heavy. My feet shivered while trying to stand, and I was completely horrified about my illusions.

"He's insane. He's crazy; Garry is always like that," I mumbled.

Garry is one of the indecent boys; delinquent once he grows up, many people said. At the age of fourteen, he had several tattoos on his body. He is hot-tempered, very aggressive, forceful, and his short height adds up with his overall character, the "Napoleon complex". My Aunt and Uncle couldn't stop him. They were trying to hide that Garry is a misbehaving child, but who can really cover up someone's not-so-good behaviour?

My Auntie Lorette kept on thinking that Garry is such a lovely boy. Uncle Paul believed that it was us who is a bad influence to his son, and of course, we have my mum who is so optimistic, repeating herself that Garry is a boy. In her own opinion, it's normal for a youngster to behave differently.

Personally, I couldn't say I like Garry. He would always steal my things, my clothes and almost everything. The most irritating part is that every time I would tell mum about what happened, she would just tell me that Garry is just like that, and would make me feel like it's my responsibility to adapt to his behaviour. He would always call me fat, but not one day that I called him little.

I don't mind those acts. I just don't want him to take my things.

Still, here I am, sitting with them eating, convincing myself that Garry is insane, and finally realise that it was him making dreadful sound for me to get scared. However, I have no idea if my understanding is proper.

He asked me why I eat so little, saying that it's not normal for me because I am fat. He asked me what's going on, and if I am frightened.

"Of course not, why must I?" I answered in a disturbed voice.

There's a lot of what ifs in the innermost part of my head:

What if he really heard the same frightening sound that I heard?

What if he knew that there was a monster under the bed?

What if it was him who was always making fun of me and scaring me?

Could he be the one?

I'm just a twelve-year-old boy. I shouldn't be bothering myself with all of these. But why?

My mum appeared behind my back and tapped my shoulder, questioning me if I don't like the food and if there's anything wrong. She thought that I'm acting like a spoiled child who doesn't want to eat what she served, and only want chips and sweets.

"What is wrong with you? What do you want?" mum's words in an annoyed tone.

"There's nothing wrong, mum," I answered.

We continued eating, and I started enjoying the food while forgetting the nightmare that I had, and what Garry was talking about.

"Everyone is having a dream. So why must I think that my bad dream is a reality? That's being insane. It's an illusion, and I have to get over with that," telling myself in silence.

Then, we started talking like normal teenage children. Mervin asked me about my studies, and Addie shared her experience at her new school. Garry stopped talking about the sounds that he heard, and instead, he just bragged about his tattoos on his body.

Chapter 2: Masterpiece on the Other Side

While reading the book, I heard a loud knock outside the door.

"Come in", I said in return.

This young lady came in to my room with an inviting smell of food. She placed it on my desk, and asked me if I need further assistance with anything. She is very gentle; she's friendly and delightful. She pony-bonded her black and thick hair that suited her innocent face, with a smile on the lips that put her own eyes together into a dazzling diamond. Her clean, purely white shirt and pants made me feel that I'm being well-taken care of. It's a pity that I couldn't even recall the name of this young lady, but I didn't bother myself to remember, either to ask her name.

She kindly asked me if she could go, and I allowed her.

I looked at my desk and saw the cloche cover on my plate. I'm excited to open it; it smells nice, and I feel hungry. Maybe because I'm reading something; well, it has a good start for me. I can't even remember the last time I read, or if I have even read books before. Who knows?

I opened my food, and was amazed because of its smell. The smell is fantastic, and I cannot explain how it looks like. It is beef minced with mashed potatoes on the top of it, and butternut on the side. I am not sure what's the name of the food, but I feel like I've tasted this before. Again, I never mind recalling the name of it, and take my first bite.

"Wow, this is lovely," I muttered.

I enjoyed every bite of it. The mince that was well cooked, the mash that complement the food's texture, the soda with three cubes of ice, and a good book to read are just the perfect things to complete your day.

I looked through my window and saw the incredible scenery in front of me- a natural landscape: mountain hills covered with tall trees and greens, the bird is flying so high that it can reach the white cloud and blue skies, the animals making sounds and the whisper of the wind that can make the leaves fly away.

One accurate picture of the word "masterpiece."

I finished my food, and is now waiting for someone to clean my table, and take my plate and cutlery away.

While waiting for them, I enjoyed looking on what is in front of me- a real perfect creation. How I wish I can run into the fields, feel the sun's heat on my skin, and feel the wind on my body, but I think it will take a while for me to do it. For now, I felt contented that I have eyes to see this beautiful scenery. I consider myself lucky because not all people can see what I can see right now; I am grateful.

The nice young lady came back, and greeted me in a cheerful manner.

"Hi! How's the food? Did you like it?" She asked.

"I loved it", I replied

She took all the things, and again, asked me if I still need anything.

"You're such a lovely lady, but nothing", I told her.

The lady walked away, and closed the door. I looked once again to the beautiful view in front of me, and opened the book, looking for where I stopped.

"I better continue reading this one," I said to myself.

"Goodbye doesn't mean the end; memories will be back once you see each other again."

The holiday is over, and it's time to say goodbye to everyone. I feel unhappy because I know it will take long years for us to see each other again. I like playing games with my cousins. I love having them around, and it makes me occupied.

I remember when I asked my Aunt Lorette if they can stay for a couple of more days; however, I felt Anthony's hand holding my shoulder really tight like he's telling me that I must close my mouth because he doesn't want them to stay for long.

"Auntie and Uncle have a lot of jobs to do, Kevin, and they need to go", my brother said.

I know, by that time, they have such good jobs, drive good cars, possess shiny pieces of jewellery and expensive things, which made me wonder why Garry needs to steal my items; maybe it's natural to him.

At my immature time, I can still remember their behaviour towards us. It is clear like water running into the river.

For such a young age, I know that not one day, they will bring something to cook every time they visit our home. They never bring gifts or presents for mum or us. Mum is the only person who will buy food for them through credits. She cooks food like there is a party for her relatives, but she couldn't even pay for it at the end of the month.

It became so hard for my mum to raise us on her own. They told me that my dad passed away because of a tragic accident when I was little. Dad fell from the stairs while he worked as a maintenance guy.

I don't have memories of my dad at all, and my brother is lucky enough that he can picture our father. All I know is that they were very close to each other; they used to play and do all the funny things while I, I can't picture him; I don't know how his appearance looks like, or how he is as a dad.

"Why do you have to buy those expensive chops and foods for them, mum? How are you going to pay it?" I always asked her that question over and over, but she would always give me one answer.

"Never mind. At least you give something."

I know mum loves her relatives so much, especially her brother, or maybe, she is just kind-hearted, and it is her way of showing partiality for them.

The last food that we have in our fridge was packed, and my mother gave it to them so that they have something to eat on their journey because it will be a long drive; they are located in Johannesburg, and we are living in Durban.

She taught me to be generous to others and expect nothing in return. She'll give whatever she has, and what can I say? That's my mum.

It is time for them to go. We gave each one of our relatives goodbye kisses and hugs. The last person that I hugged is Diana. She was just standing, not saying anything. She looks as if she is out of her mind. I hugged her as her little brother and gave her a friendly smile.

"Are you ok, Diana? Are you sad because you're living this place now?" I asked her.

"I don't want to be with this place anymore, Kevin, and I will never come back here again unless I'm dead", she whispered in my ears.

"Is it because of the monster? Did the monster scare you?" I questioned her one more time.

"Yes, Kevin. But it is more than a monster. You have to be careful, do you understand?" She added.

That's the final word that I heard from her. All that I can remember is that uncle Paul was waving his hand out of the window of the black and shiny vehicle that he was driving to say that they all need to go.

At that time, Diana's last words are still a mystery roaming in my head.

I'm standing outside thinking what Diana really meant. To be honest, I never understand what kind of feeling is now growing inside of me, yet one thing is for sure- there is something erroneous.

"Come, Kevin", I heard my brother yelled.

I came by him and asked why he needs to scream at me. My gesture and my voice's tone were initiating a fight towards him. In fact, I can no longer recall if there is one time that we bond together without having a fight or an argument about simple things. As a twelve-year-old boy, it just makes me happy every time my brother gets irritated. As I said, he's the complete opposite of me.

"What did Diana tell you?" He asked in a concerned voice.

I didn't answer him correctly, and I intend to aggravate him. "She said you are more than a monster, and I must be careful."

My answer came like a bolt from the blue. Anthony's face got disturbed, and his fist clenched and shook, wanting to punch me. And from that moment, I knew that my pun upset my brother. Maybe it was not the right time to annoy him, or annoy anyone.

I ran to my room and hid from him, like he's the monster that I'm terrified of. Nevertheless, I am the real little monster for him.

I hung around inside the four corners of my room; it is a tiny chamber for myself. My room has blue paint all over the wall. The cartoon character Bugs Bunny is imprinted on my pillow and blanket. The poster of the movie Pretty Woman with Julia Roberts is hanging on my wall, and my radio tape player is continuously playing my favourite songs by Cliff Richard, Hey Mr. Dream Maker, and Wired for Sound.

I'm waiting for the moon to bloom, and finally face the monster. The night has unfavourable prevailing conditions for me. I got scared, and overthought that the beast would take me, pull me from my bed and swallow me. So this time, I have to face my fear. I need to end this absurdity and know what Diana told me.

However, an unexpected thing happened- the monster never came.

I held back, looking into the shadow. There's no faceless monster. I stared at the other side, and all I could see is my silhouette against the gleaming moon. I bided my time, but nothing happened. There's no monster in the shadow, there's no monster under the bed, and for the second time, I dwindled myself.

"Don't let senseless imagination take your mind, Kevin", I said to myself.

I went out of my room shattered. I knew that the hallucination has been restraining me from being a normal boy, and it caused so much anguish on me. The brain inside of my head is tormented; I can feel that my body's form is not working correctly. I am slowly becoming deceptive.

"No one is going to believe me because nothing here in my mind is true. That is the fact. But what did Diana mean about her words?" Questioning myself in stillness.

And there were no answers for the hundreds of questions of mine.

I became so exhausted, and my whole soul is now looking for rest. Even so, my body is telling me to stop and sleep. I decided to look for my mum, but she is now sleeping, and I don't want to interrupt her peaceful sleep. As I went out of mum's room, I saw my brother standing and glaring at me. Anthony's eyes were full of frustration. The motion from the top to the bottom of his body gave tremendous chills all over me.

"You're insane", while looking at him, saying those words.

He's just standing like a sturdy pole, doing nothing against me. I decided to walk away and to ponder. He's very distinct from what he really is; Anthony is a man of tactical shrewdness, but the man in front of me, standing and looking, is wholly perturbed.

I heard him saying, "I'm just tired, Kevin."

I looked back and answered, "What you want me to do?"

"I want you to be quiet just for once. Do it for me, Kevin." He replied and left me hanging.

From that moment, I realised one thing, and it is messing around me.

I shattered myself because of my delusion and, at the same time, my immaturity is hurting my brother and family. I rattled Anthony's cage. Maybe I'm too much, too childish that I couldn't understand that I'm hurting him. At last, I realised that I seriously need to stop.

Chapter 3: Coming of Age

"This is a good story. I wonder who put this book here?" Asking myself while I'm in the middle of reading.

The work is expressive, and it's convincing me that I have to carry on reading. I was enjoying every page, but sadly, someone came and stood up at the back of me. I turned around and saw a rangy and good-looking guy. He has reading glasses on his round shiny eyes. He is wearing a long white coat with black long-sleeved polo and pants below.

Then he started to ask, "How are you, Mister? How's your feeling?"

I'm focusing on his face, reading every gesture, from his eyes, hand, and body. His voice is like a melody playing stunningly, and his smile, manifesting so much care that is drawn on his face, makes me feel that there's something inaccurate.

I don't like him.

"You are looking good today", he added.

My eyes were stuck trying to understand every single thing about him.

He gives me different feelings- feelings that I cannot explain, which no one will like. I can sense my weak bones within me. I start to quiver.

"I don't like you", I said.

"I know, you told me things more than that", he responded.

He talked a lot about himself, telling things I don't want to hear. This man was trying to motivate and elevate himself in front of me. His smile showed malevolence, and lastly, tried to show concern towards me that I couldn't even believe.

He grinned like a Cheshire Cat. He never opposed neither tried to ask me why I don't like him. He's different, and it's wrong for me. I looked at him in a demented and dizzy way, but he never said anything, not even one word. He knows me. He is knowledgeable about me, and I can sense it. I don't know if there is something wrong with him or is it me that is using my mind too much to interpret his character.

He turned around and said, "They are going to give you medication later; I want you to take it."

"For what? I am good," I responded.

"It's for you, sir. Have a good day ahead." Then he left.

This man tried to be warm towards me. Still, it is my instinct that doesn't like him. I don't want to bother myself just to adore anyone. I am aware that we all have a soft spot for most people, but I literally lost it this time. Not for a moment that he did something to displease me;

however, my instinct is telling me not to like him. The rhythm of his voice is not genuine for me, and his smile on his charming face is an absolute mystery. Furthermore, I carry on telling myself that I wasn't born to appreciate every single person in front of me. It is my decision anyway.

I took the book and looked for where I stop.

I feel like reading this fiction is persuading me to continue scrutinising every part of it. I did not think highly of this; the appearance of this one is unpleasant. Somebody wrote a book with no cover, no title, and no author's name, and it seems to be fallen apart, but I am starting to like it more and more.

"Here it is. This is the part where I stopped"

And I continue.

"We cannot stop the coming of time, but wasting it will be a future crime."

Five years passed by, and everything changed. I feel like the untroubled milieu of the place where I grew is now different. The neighbourhood where I grew up is now diverse from each other. Aside from that, people behave like strangers. The old faces of the city became unfamiliar to each other. For others, it can be baffling, but for me, it is maturity- a coming of age to everyone.

My brother Anthony is now a full-time father at the age of twenty-one. He met his wife Alexa close to our place. She is beautiful and young.

Alexa's appearance is stunning; she is leggy with long shiny ginger hair. The sunlight is revealing her porcelain skin, and her body is glass-hour shaped. Other than that, she is not just glamorous; she is very loving towards my brother and their baby girl.

I am a living witness to my brother's success. In every single way, Alexa taught him things that he can use to build for their future. Both of them started from scratch- sweating blood and breaking their bones- but the hard work has now paid off.

He and his wife are successful entrepreneurs: meeting wealthy businessman, making good deals about money, negotiating with the most people, and travelling to different countries.

I can say that Alexa thought of him a lot. She built Anthony's confidence and taught him how to talk, charm, and close deals about people's investments. He got things that everybody wants in life. His lovely car, prodigious house, wealth, intelligence, strong wife and adorable daughter are the things that can define the word "success."

It is a lovely future for both of them.

Anthony's life transformation is mind-blowing. Aside from his financial status, his standpoint and approach in life are out-of-common. He is entirely different from who he was to his family. From a soft-spoken child, he became ill-tempered, arrogant, overbearing, and more than that, from a well-mannered and respectful son, he suddenly became impudent to mum, but not to everyone. He chooses who to respect and who should not. I never saw him act like this in front of his business partner, or people driving a worth-a-million car. He's always humble and sweet with them, appearing like he can't even hurt a fly.

It's still taking part in my head how brusque he was to our mum, giving her uncomplimentary remarks, and talking bad about us. I saw how mum hurt, but she never did anything. She keeps on loving Anthony; she's taking care of my brother's child, but in the end, my brother would just be shutting her off. It seems like he wants our mother breathless. He became greedy and mercenary.

"I'm sorry, mama," I said

"She's to blame, Kevin. It's all Alexa," she replied

My mum was in despair at that time, asking herself what happened to her beloved son. But then again, she would deny it. She's blaming Alexa why Anthony's behaviour changed. She repudiates the fact that it was Anthony's fault, and not anyone else's. Well, who can actually blame her? She's a mother, and any mother, seeing their most-loved son showing his ungracious side, will definitely cause a heartbreak.

Mum loves Anthony so much that Alexa is her defence mechanism for every bad thing that is going on with my brother. She should always tell me that if Anthony never met Alexa, and if Alexa never taught him wrong things, then he is not going to change; he'll still be a down-to-earth and loving son. However, I know the truth. He's like that not only to mum, but also to his own wife- the wife who helps him grow and achieve things, the wife who supports each thing about him, and the wife who loves his flaws and everything.

I can't blame Alexa for his faultiness; I know it is merely him.

Alexa loves him so much, to the point that she never cares about other people, or even us. She can do impossible things for Anthony, and she believes that my brother is the centre of her life.

I know because I was there. I saw what was happening between the two of them, between Alexa and my brother.

It is common for mum to ask me to visit my brother and take care of my brother's child because Anthony doesn't want relatives around. And of course, as a seventeen-year-old boy, I cannot complain or say a word, so I did. I was always in his huge house. He has a fancy silver gate that, once it opens up, will lead you to a long, secluded driveway going to his garage where his fleet of luxury cars are parked. There are Lamborghini, Ferrari, Benz, and Porsche, amongst others.

They lived in a triple storey mansion with a pool on top. The wall has big expensive paintings. The chandelier gives graciousness in every part of his house's interior, and the most beautiful things are the windows in each room, overlooking the mountain and the ocean.

I wasn't there as a family. I was there as a normal worker, looking after the child, and cutting grass on his ten thousand square meter yard.

Mum said that he is different now, but he never changed his behaviour to me because of his money; he wants me to be quiet and give him peace. At that moment, I thought it was only for that night, but my brother never told me that he wants it for a bit longer.

I know that he changed, from that night, towards me. He never considered me as a brother from that time. I already felt a quantum leap on us five years ago.

After cleaning Anthony's colossal yard, I would sit on a big stone at the back of his house where the kitchen is. I would sit for a couple of minutes, burning myself under the sun. I love the feeling of the sun hitting on my warm toast skin for no reason.

The smell of Alexa's food reminds me of how empty my stomach is. It makes me feel so excited to go back home to my mum so that I can eat. I know that they will not be giving me anything, not even a glass of drink. I go inside their house just to say that I need to go back home. Anthony would provide me with seventy Rands, while I was thinking that it's for my transportation, and hoping that he would pay me at the end of the month, which he didn't.

He keeps on telling people that he would help us in everything, even in financial means, but he never did it. We never asked for anything, not even one cent. He never gave us anything.

After an exhausting trip, I am back home. I see mum waiting for me and trying to find a new story about my brother. I never lied to her. I told her what I did the whole day long, and what they did for me.

"Money changes people, doesn't it, son?" She asked.

I responded in a dejected sound.

"No, mum, you are wrong. Money doesn't change people. It just simply shows their colour and intentions."

I ate the food that Mum made for me, and went to my room, trying to rest my ill-used body. My eyes slowly closed 'til I don't know what happened next.

■■■

I remember one night when something woke me up from my deepest sleep in the middle of darkness. I felt debilitated and scared at the same time.

I have never gone through this way for so long. I bore this feeling many years ago. I thought I was having a nightmare again, a bad night, or maybe, delusion after five years. I thought it was back. My fear, my weakness, my illusion was now right inside my room, inside of me. I closed my eyes, trying to be brave and not feel scared, convincing myself that I'm old enough to see what is real and what delusions are.

Sadly, it did not help me. It didn't ease the pain.

I could feel him, the faceless monster moving around, playing. He was here, enjoying in exasperating my mind, and doing his best to make my cold blood run. I was stuck with my fear five years ago, and there's no other way that I can escape from it. I am still a twelve-year-old juvenile boy who doesn't know to perceive things, and can't help myself.

I took some guts, and looked at him; he was not a faceless monster anymore. I could see his eyes looking at me in anguish, wanting to hurt me, wanting me dead, wanting to swallow me, and I didn't have any idea what I could do to wake up from this horrible dream. I wanted somebody to help me, but no one could. It's within me, within my brain messing me up and stopping me from being ordinary. I got exhausted and left all the feelings behind.

I closed my eyes, frightened, and said; "I just have to live with it". Then, I slept.

Chapter 4: Bloodline Stop

I heard a soft voice calling me, saying, "Sir, here's your medication. Please take this; it will help you" It is the same young lady who assisted me a while ago.

I asked her who's that tall and handsome man who came to me, and she told me that he is the one who was helping me to get well.

"Why do I need to take that medicine?" I asked out of curiosity.

"Because it can help you", she answered.

I can't remember what happened to me and how I got here. I don't know this place either. The only thing that I know is that I am sitting in this room painted in white.

"Why I can't remember everything? Where am I? I can't even remember what happened this morning?" That time, I noticed that my voice is rising in distress.

"Usually, most patients who been through a trauma forget things; it is completely normal. But the good thing is that reading will help you to remember things slowly. So go on, and continue reading." She responded.

I don't know where I am, and I can't remember things. It feels like I am drifting in the air out of nowhere. Then, this young lady smiled at me; her smile seems to tell me that I will start remembering things soon. She's telling me that everything will be fine.

"One thing that I realised working here is that you cannot save people from themselves. It's either they will figure it out or not." She said.

"But if you drink your medication, if you are going to help yourself, then you will start to get better. And, the most important thing is that you'll eventually start remembering things about you." She added, and then she walked away.

For some reasons, I trust her. I took a deep breath, and calmed myself down. I stopped thinking for a moment, telling myself that if I help and encourage myself, my brain will gradually start to remember who I am and who I was before.

It is a small white container, and there are two caplets inside. I took the medicines that they gave me, pinning my hope on them. There's no way I can help myself but to do it anyway. I get to hold of what I am reading, and listen to this lady.

Once again, I opened the book, and started reading from where I stopped.

"Human must take a breath like a lover, or live like a beast."

I heard my brother calling me while I was cleaning outside; my whole body was dripping with sweat, and my smell was like decomposing grass, a stinky-swamp. My hands and nails were covered with earth. I really didn't see myself being like this, but this is the out-turn of the only room given to me- an opportunity as a garden boy.

My features are completely different from what it was. My flawless skin is now painfully burned and enclosed by a rash. My plump body is now skinny, and no one can even compare my face now and when I was young. My clothes are old, and I don't know how to dress up. Imagine, from being a spoiled boy, I am currently working in a yard.

I walked towards him, and he looked at me from head to toe, probably because of how I looked. He asked me to open his automated gate; it was under maintenance, so the only way that it could be opened was by doing it manually. I was shocked when I saw mum standing outside, waiting for the gate to open.

"What are you doing here, mum?" I asked in annoyance.

"I want to visit your brother and my granddaughter", she replied.

My mind can't reach the idea of how mum took a journey using public transportation just to see my brother. The distance of our home from Anthony is unquestionably draining. We need to take three to four taxis that are overloaded with different kinds of people: old, young, sick, healthy, kind and dangerous. The smell of the town's crowded place is vile; the site is grimy, and the area's happenings are absolutely mucky.

Finally, after a long trip, the taxi driver will drop us off at our designated stations.

Over the succeeding travels to a crowded place, now it is time to face the kilometres walk. It begins at the bus station, and leads up to Anthony's house. The heat and weariness can easily damage us. Those are what mum needs to go through just to see Anthony: an aged woman wanting to see her treasured son.

"It is not safe for you to travel, mama. You are old for this", I complained.

"I'm fine, son", she answered.

I walked with Mum going inside Anthony's house. She saw him sitting on his cosy Kalahari leather lounge suit. She smiled full of love to him, but I knew that he wouldn't like it.

"What are you doing here? I never asked you to come here." He raised his voice to mum.

"I never do anything wrong with you, and I don't know what happened to you, Anthony." Mum said while her tears were cascading down to her cheeks.

"You knew what happened to me, and you never did anything. Is it because I am not your bioligical child?"

 Get out from here, and take your terrible son," He added.

Anthony was full of anguish; his eyes turned red like there's a demon wanting to come out. I could see the vein on his head running to his neck. His jaw clenched just like his fist. I don't know what's the reason for his grudge towards us. He was sitting on the way that he could just stand easily and hurt mum or me, and in the end, he did. He pulled the carpet where mum was standing; as a result, mum hit the floor.

"You are out of your mind. Why do you need to do that?" I howled at him while helping our mother to get up.

Mum stared at Anthony in grief, and asked him why.

"You don't know how hard it was growing up in lack and shortage. You don't have any idea how terrible it is working just to help you and your helpless Kevin because no one is going to do that for the both of you."

"You don't know how painful it was seeing your own mother keeping quiet about what happened, and it has been continuously messing me while growing up, so please go and take your younger son- an immature, spoiled and hopeless child." He added.

We were lost for words by that time. I was voiceless. Mum and I looked at Anthony, and couldn't say even a word. I hold mum's hand, shaking and guiding her while going out from his house. Mum was hurt, so am I?

Anthony is self-deceptive. He's mentioning things that never happened. He was saying that he helped us, but I couldn't remember or see. Yes, he is the responsible son to upkeep our home, and that's it. He helped mum to do housework, but mum was the one who supported us financially and gave us security, not him. Not once that he gave mum something because he never wanted it. He's telling us that mum never did anything, but that is not true, because she raised us very well.

I looked back at him and asked, "You cannot use us because we don't have money, can you, Anthony?"

"No, Kevin. Every time I see your face, I know that you are going to wreck me. Your intrusiveness will ruin me, so you better leave." He answered.

We continued walking, leaving my brother's house. Our minds were in no place, flying somehow. Not for a moment that mum and I would think that our life is too much for him. I was trying to understand him. I tried to understand that growing up without a father, and acting as a father would never be easy for a young boy. In addition to that, living with an immature child like me cannot be called life. Maybe, Anthony is right; I'm ruining him. I'm not his son, and I'm not my brother's responsibility.

The person I knew who was ruined at this point was mum. We reached home but she was still crying. I don't know how to stop her or calm her down, and all I could do was hug her.

"I'm still here mama. Don't cry." Until she fell asleep.

It was the longest day for me, and it might also be long for anyone else. Just visualise seeing your mother's face bearing the expression of hopelessness. My brother's inflamed behaviour might have given me a million reason to run out of steam, but I handled it. I lay down on my bed smoothly. There's someone beside me, and it made me feel thrilled and delighted at the same time because I never got scared and never asked myself who was that.

He wasn't hiding under the bed. He was sleeping right next to me.

Chapter 5: Reality to Be Experienced

As the years go by, I learned how to stretch and even break my bone. I worked as a packer in one of the biggest supermarkets in our town in Durban. Every night, I would work as a construction worker, lifting heavy objects with my skinny body. I can't count using my fingers how many strenuous jobs I did. Different jobs, different pains, and different places, but the same low salary; I was earning three hundred and sixty Rands a week if I was lucky enough.

I remember how I should separate all the rotten vegetables like potatoes, carrots and lettuce from the fresh ones; the smell of rotten vegetables can be compared to a dead rat full of fly. Sometimes I wanted to puke, but if I did, I would lose my job. I felt embarrassed every time my school friends would laugh at me in public while doing that kind of work.

"Hey man, how's the smell going?" My friends, screaming in public, and laughing at me.

It left me speechless.

The most dreadful situation I faced was working in a cold storage room where they stock all the citrus fruits awaiting to be exported; the room was three-degree Celsius. I was wearing thick clothes like I was living in Antarctica. I should arrange the boxes, put them in the right places, and dust them with the help of three more men.

Eight to ten hours of working in a cold storage room was like working in a place of torture. I could feel my blood getting cold, and my hand starting to freeze. Most of the time, I was going out of the cold storage walking like a zombie. All of the joints in my body were locked. Some people intimidated me, indicating that working in freezing temperature would stop me from having a child, but I didn't believe in that kind of story. I brushed it off.

I wasn't proud of my job, yet I am pleased with myself. At the end of the month, I would get back home with something for mum. I would give her my salary inside the envelope, unopened. I love sharing it with her, and it makes me happy that I could help her in a small way. I am always excited for mum to open my salary sealed even though how little it was because I'm sure that she would appreciate it.

Another best thing about working so hard was that my body was way too exhausted that I would just eat and go to sleep right away. There were no nightmares, no fears and no monster for years.

But the reality is not all the time is a good time.

I believe that people will always have their bad day in their lives. I lost my job working in a cold room because of the three men working there. Until now, I can still feel the pain right inside of me. One day, I got irritated at them. I was doing the job, and the three of them were sitting and laughing. I asked them nicely to help me, but their reaction shocked me, and made my spirit ran away.

My heart stopped for a few seconds, asking my mind what have I done.

They stood from where they were sitting, and started to punch me on my face and stomach. Two of the workers were holding my arms, and the biggest man kept knocking me on my face and body. The last thing that I remember was the sound of my bones, cracked. I woke up in severe pain, and I was at home with mum. She helped me to get up, and her face was full of concern.

"You cannot go back to that place again Kevin, you will die. They are wild". She begged.

I answered in a bantered way, "You're just frightened that you will not see your future grandchild, mum? That's what people say," I responded and laughed.

After a couple of months sitting and not having a job, I took my old mobile device; it was a keypad model. I started to phone our relatives, and I first tried to call Mervin and Addie, but they never answered. They are probably living now in Australia. The last person I tried to reach was my Uncle Paul, and luckily, he responded to my call when I dialled his number. I gave the phone to mum, and they began to talk.

Mum was so happy that she finally got to spoke with her brother, and before they ended their conversation, I asked mum if she could hand me the phone to speak to my cousins. Willy is the one who managed to talk to me. We talked a lot, we asked things about each other, and it ended up with me asking if he could organise a job, even in a minor position, for me. My heart was so glad when he told me to come to their home, and they would give me a work.

■■■

On the next day, I got up and moved early before the sunrise. I travelled from Durban going to Johannesburg, finding fortune. It was six hours of travel. After that, I sat and waited in the bus station for my relatives to pick me up. After a couple of minutes, I saw mum's brother, Paul, driving the same black car that he was driving eight years ago. I can still remember.

He drove back home, and for so many years, I met all of them again. Uncle Paul and Auntie Lorette still looked the same considering the years since the last time I saw them. At this present moment, both of them are raising their seven-year-old daughter. Her name is Sunny. The name already explained so much about her; she is a very cute, cheerful, and lovely child. Aside from that, she has curly blonde hair, cat eyes and a milky white complexion. I also saw Garry at my Auntie's house. He was staying there. His appearance looked more proper and neat compare to before.

I asked about Mervin and Addie, but they were no longer in South Africa. My intuition was correct; they moved with their parents to Australia, so the communication stopped between families.

In addition to that, I asked them where Diana was, and they couldn't give me an answer. They told me that Diana left them seven years ago, and she told them that she wanted to live and build on her own life. I asked my Aunt and Uncle if there was a way that I could reach or contact Diana, but unfortunately, they had zero communication with her. Uncle Paul told me that one day, Diana woke up, and decided to go. Based on their story, Diana's changes were tremendous. She was coming home late, smelling of alcohol and allowing different men to go inside their house. At that time, she was at her legal age, so my Auntie let her do what she wanted, and allowed her to go.

"You don't need to look for her. She must be living her life now," Garry said.

" I'm still looking forward seeing her again," I replied

On the other side, Willy was no longer living with them. He was living three blocks away from Aunt Lorette and Uncle Paul's house.

He is already married, the same as my brother Anthony. Willy is now a father of a six-year-old child. He looks much older than before. And when I hugged him, he smelled of alcohol. I met his lovely daughter Nadia; she is adorable and respectful to visitors, and I'm sure that she learned it from her mother. Willy's wife, named Elaine, is very polite. She served food, asked what I want, and was very kind. After talking about my personal life for the past years, I opened up the conversation about the job that Willy organised for me. My Aunt and Uncle own a company for local community newspapers, and all of them are managing their family business. He told me that I would maintain the cleanliness of printing machines and all the electronic equipment for the newspapers. I knew it would be a lot easier, unlike before.

"Why can't you just stay with us? Here in this house, we still have one vacant room, and you can pay half of the price than pay the full cost somewhere else. You just need to get your stuff like groceries and toiletries". Willy offered.

They made me aware that the salary was not too high, so I grabbed the opportunity of living with them. They asked me to sleep in their spare room, and I can use and pay half for it as long as I'm working in their company.

I was so grateful, and said thousands of thankful words. The job might be so far from my mother, but I know that I can do something to help her. I was looking forward to my waiting duties. I gave assurance to every one of them that I would do my best to be efficient in my job. I got up early in the morning, prepared myself and headed off to the workplace. I decided to get a taxi on my own because I don't want to ask anyone for a ride, and bother them in the end. As I arrive at the factory, Uncle Paul showed me how to do and run mechanical contrivances. I thought it would be trouble-free because all that I needed to do was to maintain the machine's cleanliness. I never had any idea of how big my task was, until I saw not one, but many printing machines.

One thing that I learned was no manual job will be free and easy. You have to bend, hurt yourself and break your body. Sometimes, my whole spirit and embodiment were so tired that I missed where the right station of my relative's place was. I got lost while sleeping in the taxi. I was new to the area and still taking my time to memorise the whole travel. When I continued moving and almost reached my cousin's home, tired and dying, I saw a burgundy car parked right in front of the property where my Uncle and Auntie stayed three blocks away from their son, Willy. I looked closely, and I noticed that my Aunt Lorette stepped out of the vehicle. She reached in through the driver seat window, and gave the stranger a goodbye kiss. My Auntie didn't see that I was walking from afar. She went inside her house, and I never got the chance to see the stranger's face.

"It must be her friend", I said to myself.

I came back to my cousin's home, restless. I could feel that every part of me was maltreated. I ate the leftover in the kitchen, had a nice warm bath, and went straight to my room to lie down and sleep on my bed. I was blaming myself for what was going on in my life. If I thought about my future, and gave importance to my education when I was a little bit younger, I am sure that I would never experience this kind of pain. No company wanted to hire me because of my school record. However, I kept on saying that one day, I don't have to feel this way. I will find a way to break free from my bittersweet life. Time will come that I will use my mouth, charm and pen to make money. All I need is someone who will give me a chance to prove myself. I'm trying to convince and lift my confidence that I am more than this. I just don't have the opportunity to prove myself, and I'm patiently waiting for it.

■■■

It was the year 1973, the seventh of June. My life every morning and night was the same day by day. There's nothing new for me. The same old life: get up early, do tremendous work, go back home, feel the pain and rest.

The same night, same pain, and same question;

"When will I get away with my troubled and tormented life? When will I stop myself being slave", while closing my eyes.

Chapter 6: Nightmare after Years

I fold the upper right corner of the page where I stopped, and put the book away. I never take the chance to remember the page number; I am not good at memorising things. I rest for a while and look around; the room is painted with off-white colour, the bedding is spotless, and the whole place is polished.

"Nice, I'm in the hospital. But I don't even know what happened to me", I said to myself.

I wasn't able to recall things concerning what is going on about me, my family, and what happened throughout this morning. All I can remember is that I was reading and spending my time while positioned in the wheelchair. I attempted to move my legs, but without success. My lower limbs were numb; they were senseless. I was absolutely hit in panic. My situation was disturbing, and I wanted to scream. But I chose to be calm.

"I'll wait for an answer. These people will tell me what happened," I whispered.

I'm almost into the midway of reading, but it doesn't help in any way. Nothing at all. They told me that it would help slowly, so I resumed, and read from where I stopped.

"The monster lies inside our head. It is not hiding under our bed."

I've been working for many months with my uncle and auntie's business. The job was not that easy, different from what I expected. I should clean every single part of giant printing machines, and get one thousand six hundred Rands a month. I understood that it was not so big, but I was glad.

I was sending mum money, and paying accommodation to my cousin every month. And after all the expenses, I tried my best to save for myself. I kept my belt really tight.

After a long time saving some cash from my salary, I eventually purchased a new phone. My first device was very old and needed to be restored, which would cause a lot more silver.

To a certain extent, my mobile phone helped me. For a little while, it released all my exhaustion and temporarily relaxed my mind. I could speak to mum whenever I had a chance. I would always ask her how's her day, and my heart was fulfilled every time she's telling me that she's doing fine. Other than that, I could also write my story for a moment. I didn't have time to talk about my suffering or stress to anyone, so I preferred to put it down on my own.

While at work, I realised that for the past few weeks, Willy has only been appearing every weekend; he was staying at home on weekdays, and was drinking his whisky the whole day and night. His wife Elaine was the one who's working for them. She would come home at night, and do all the chores inside the house. No doubt that my cousin Willy was living his life.

Willy began to take care of Nadia. However, I was able to grasp things pretty quickly; I could see that there was a big difference between how Elaine and Willy raised their daughter. Many months ago, Nadia was a playful child; she was smiling and laughing a lot with her mum, but now she became quiet. She didn't want to talk, and was always hiding in her room like a mute.

One day I asked Willy about his daughter, "She is not used to you; she likes her mum so much, doesn't she?"

"Part of getting bigger, Kevin." He answered.

I stopped minding what I noticed about Nadia. Her father was right; it was part of growing up. It was still playing in my head what happened to Anthony and me when both of us were getting older together. When I was a little boy, all I wanted to do was to play all the time. Our mum spoiled me, but now, I have to work on my own. When Anthony was in his teenage years, he was so close to our mother, but he never wanted us to be around when he got his own life. That is the reality and the sad part of human life.

▪▪▪

It was a Saturday morning, and I didn't need to go to work. I rested the whole day, and never noticed that the time passed by. I went out of my room, and saw Willy drinking his alcohol.

"How are you Will? Where's Elaine?"

"She's finishing things at work", he responded.

I went to the kitchen, and cooked my own meal for the night. I offered my cousin to eat with me, but he refused, saying that he was heavily loaded with food. After eating, I went back to my room, and opened my phone. I dialled my mum's number, and we talked for an hour. I was satisfied and happy hearing her voice, and knowing that she was in excellent condition. I set aside everything and lay down. I closed my eyes gradually, thanking my body for being strong while doing a strenuous and backbreaking task. This must be the payback of what I did when I was young. At that time, I started to play truant at school, and my academic grades were disrupted. I was skipping curriculums, and didn't spend time respecting my studies. And, as a result, the workplace also has no respect for me.

The next thing that happened was I woke up in fear. My room was swollen by blackness, and the deafening silence drove me crazy and forced me to ask where I was.

"This must be hell", I answered to myself.

The terror of this night was indistinguishable from what I felt a decade ago. It was Christmas time, and the memories of mine left clear and unclouded.

I heard the cry and the groan once again in the blink of an eye. It was not just the monster right next to me; it was the same faceless monster who scared the hell out of Diana and me many years back.

My eyes were wide open, looking around, but I couldn't see a thing. It wasn't functioning well; however, my ears could hear the wailing of someone, and my body could feel the grumbling all over the house.

"I am too old for all of this. I shouldn't have horrific hallucinations." I said to myself.

I turned around on the other side of the bed, and let out a long sigh of despair. I kept on telling myself that I was stronger than before because I was no longer a child. It was a dream, and I had to let things go. Afterwards, I rested as if nothing scared me.

■■

I woke up feeling tired and a little lethargic; no doubt that it's because of the previous night. I was not too fond when my sleep was getting interrupted, but I couldn't even blame anyone. As a grown-up man, I notice that I was still having horror sleep like a child. It was not a nice feeling. It was my fault.

After having a bath, I saw Elaine and Willy, as well as their daughter, eating. Elaine asked me to come and eat with them, so I did. Time passed by, and everyone was quiet. No one wanted to begin a discussion, which gave me the impression that something wrong was going on.

"How's your night, Will?" I asked.

"It was okay", he answered

"And you, Elaine?"

"Tiring. I came home late", she responded.

Elaine looked at her daughter, Nadia, and started to ask questions, but she got no reply. Nadia's head was down, and she didn't want to look at us. I thought that maybe, Nadia had a bad night too.

"I know what happened. She's having a bad day. I used to be like that," I said.

Willy peculiarly looked at me. I could feel that he was intrigued about my words, and what they meant. If only he is the kind of person that can only understand, and would not laugh at a man that is frightened of his nightmare, then maybe there's a slight chance for me to share what I felt and what I've been going through. Still, I know that he would just make fun of me, and he's definitely going to tell me that I was insane to feel scared about dreams.

Day after day, Willy's behaviour remained the same. He was staying at home drinking whiskey, and taking care of his daughter, while Elaine was going to work the whole week, and coming home late at night. Their daughter's behaviour changed suddenly. I assumed that Nadia missed her mum, and she didn't want her dad to be at home. There was a time when I saw my cousin disciplining his child, which was completely opposite to his wife. I never saw Elaine scold or yell; she spoiled her child so much. For Elaine, Nadia will always be her small girl.

I could see in Nadia's eyes the fear and sadness. She truly needed her mum.

I couldn't say anything or give an opinion; she was their child, and I was just staying there as a worker.

I could hear the child crying in the other room. Her father was so upset to the point that I could hear him screaming. That's how he raised his child, and I didn't have any business about it; I had to mind my own.

The most disastrous circumstance that I have ever faced is my own battle every night. My mind was set waking up in the middle of the darkness asking myself if I was delusional. I could not sleep without me having terror and question in my head if I were in hell or not. I would always talk in silence that the monster who was causing the sound of despair was just an imagination. I was convinced by myself that nothing was true; in that way, it put my mind in a safe place. It helped me close my eyes slowly while looking at the beast that my brain created long ago.

One day, I came home from work, and saw my cousin, Willy, waiting outside my room. He was standing there, and gave me a friendly smile.

"Can I have a word, Kevin?" He asked.

"Sure, about what?" I responded.

He told me that I could no longer stay with them. I asked him if I did something that they never liked, or maybe I was a burden for some reason, but he gave me different explanations. He said that his wife would be using the room as an office shortly, and there was no other room for me to stay in, which meant that I have to move out as soon as possible.

I felt shattered and terrible at that time. I couldn't even say a word, yet I respected his decision. I looked worn out, and I didn't know where to go. I don't have family or friends aside from them. It's just devastating.

I've been thinking for a couple of minutes when all of a sudden, he knocked on the door. Willy came inside the room, and talked to me.

"I spoke to mum, asked her if you can stay with her, and she told me that the house is open for you", he said.

"Thank you so much, Will", I replied.

I felt awful that night; however, my mood changed when I found out that I still have a place to stay. I couldn't blame him because it was his house, and it would be his decision whatever he wanted to do, so I understood.

Later that night, I packed all my clothes and personal things; I was ready to move now. I expressed my gratitude towards Willy for keeping me and having me around. I wanted to wait for Elaine to say my appreciation, but he told me that his wife would be late as always.

I looked at Nadia; she's no longer the child that I first saw. She's not cheerful and playful anymore. I knew that she needed her mum; she loved her mum so much.

"I'm going now, Nadia", I said.

She just looked into my eyes, and never gave me a response.

Her dad answered me saying, "She's a spoiled child Kevin, and she needs to be trained. You can go now."

I left his house, and started to walk, going to my auntie and uncle's home that was just three blocks away. I stopped thinking about his child. I guess I have to think about myself now.

Chapter 7: Behind Closed Doors

After leaving Willy's house, my Auntie Lorette opened her doors for me. They didn't have a spare room, but they told me that their daughter Sunny and son Garry could be together in one place. All I needed was to do the same-pay half for my room every month, and buy my own stuffs like groceries and toiletries. I couldn't explain how thankful I was to them. They organised a job for me, and let me stay in their home. For me, having a roof for the night was more than enough.

It's not a different ambience. I would wake up early, and head off to work. My auntie and uncle were also going to work, while Garry was staying at home to take care of Sunny.

After a long day, the only rest that I have was sitting inside the congested taxi. Once I reached my relative's house, I had to cook food for myself. I didn't want to bother anyone. If I had energy, I was trying to wash my own clothes, so I didn't have to do it at the end of the week. It was always exhausting, but I had to go through this.

While having personal time, I would always write the stories and events that took place around me. I would listen to Cliff Richard's music on the radio on my phone, and sometimes, record my voice. These were the things that saved me from grey.

All of these were inadequate. Whatever I was doing before, closing my eyes, didn't provide ease. I could still feel the beast wandering throughout the house. I could still hear the sound of pain and helplessness during the dark hours. The monster was right inside this place, and I was the only one who could feel it. My senses were wide open, or maybe, I was the only person who was not in a proper disposition. It was the same old feeling. I had the chance and the power to confront and fight this mind a long time ago, but I never did; now, I am suffering.

■■■

The day dawned crisp and clear, and the sun was cresting the horizon. But instead of hearing the roosters' reverberations on the street, what I heard was Sunny's screeching. Garry was scolding and miscuing his sister more than what I can imagine. He looked like a wife-beater, battering his helpless spouse.

I could see that Garry was a kind of authoritative person. His sister was sobbing, and it seemed like he couldn't hear anything.

"Is Sunny okay?" I asked anxiously.

"She's behaving like some spoiled-brat child; we need to give her a lesson", he answered.

As I said, it was not a different ambience. Garry and Willy had the same way of looking after a child, and, as a result, the same trauma for Nadia and Sunny. The outrageous effects of disciplining were indistinct between the two. When I looked at them, they had helpless eyes, the same sound of wailing, and even the gestures didn't have differences. Before I left Willy's house, Nadia became timid, avoiding people, and always hiding in her room, which were the same behaviours that I noticed in Sunny. Different home but similar aura.

I wanted to say something, but their own father did not do anything about it. It was the same everyday story. Uncle Paul was just keeping quiet about how Garry was treating his sister that way. He'd come home early, and see the poor child crying, but he'd rush to his room quickly like he never saw it. He would lock up his room, waiting for my auntie Lorette, and not going to say one word to his son and daughter.

My auntie was not there. Whatever the circumstances were, she would come late, just like Elaine who was busy running their family business. How I wish that they'd be home too soon so that they could see what was happening to their child. I hope they could do something.

I never had a voice to speak, nor stood for the children. And if I only had, I am sure that I would not use it to say a single word. I didn't have the rights either. It was their decision about how they wanted to run their respective home, and how they were going to regulate each one of them. If I could not stand their way of disciplining a child, I have to close my eyes on my own.

I did what I needed to do, not the thing that I wanted to. I wanted to say or do something about what I could see, but I needed to keep quiet. I was the one who needed a place to stay, not them.

One late night, I saw the same burgundy car where my auntie Lorette stepped off a month ago. Now, it was right inside their property. I walked straight to their house, and I saw two new faces sitting on the couch. My relatives had unfamiliar visitors. One of them dropped off auntie that night, but I don't know which one.

While I was walking towards my room, I heard uncle Paul called my name. I looked back, and stood in front of them. He introduced me to their visitors formally. They were husband and wife.

"Seat with us," Paul said.

I was sitting right next to them, looking and listening while they were having a conversation. I noticed that my aunt and uncle were so close to their visitors. I could see how they looked at each other. The man was full of happiness in his eyes while looking at my aunt Lorette. However, for me, it's not just happiness; it is a concupiscent way of glaring, a glare of a man that needed to be looked upon.

Then their conversation stopped.

My time came that night, and I chose not to remember their names. All I could recall was the wound that was left on me; their visitors' judgement really impaired my hope in life.

Right after they completed their discussion regarding themselves, they began to ask personal questions about my existence as a human being. I have to admit that I am not intelligent enough to answer. Both of them were laughing and denigrating my way of living. Moreover, my looks became the source of their happiness for a moment.

The man told me that I should have a good job and not live in somebody else's house at the age of twenty-three. His wife was insulting my physical appearance, and mocking my style of dressing up.

"You looked like a tramp. Next time, use nicer clothes", the old woman said.

"He will never afford it; he earns so less", her husband added.

My eyes and heart became so heavy. I was holding my tears not to fall from my eyes, but my heart was already grieving. I could not say a word. I was in a state of embarrassment. Their names were removed from my brain, but their features were pictured in my memory. The woman who chattered the way I look didn't show any considerable or impressive part of her own appearance. She's an average woman, not so pretty, and not so plain, but her man had an undeniably imposing feature. He looked like Sunny, actually. He had blue slit eyes, a sharp nose, pink lips, flawless skin tone and crimped blonde hair. Their looks were clear on my head, just like the pain that they caused me.

No one stood up for me; my auntie's and uncle's mouth were closed, and Garry seemed to be happy about it. I was incapable of helping myself. I was so weak, and no one lent their hands for me. If my mum were here, I'm sure she would help me, or maybe not, just to keep the peace for everyone.

I went to my room, and lay down in agony. My body was in cruel torture, and the emotional hurt was bitterly cold. It was an unreasonable pain, a nasty and unforgettable episode of my life. I asked the wind in front of me about what I did in my life, but I got no answer. After a while of mourning, I heard from the outside my room that the old couple left the house, and at last, I managed to breathe. I let the tears flow, and I began to whimper.

If I could only go back to the time when I was studying, I promise that I would do better. Maybe it would make some differences, significant or not. If I had good academic grades, then it probably changed my condition today.

From a child that was pampered and coddled, I am now experiencing the bittersweet of life. This chapter immensely changed my existence.

The night had passed, and I went to my workplace. I cleaned everything in the factory. I decided to move fast for the reason that I wanted to get back home as quickly as I could, and rest.

After doing my duties, I took a taxi, then walked almost passing my cousin's house. I wanted to visit them, but their door was closed, so I decided to leave and go straight to my uncle's place.

I opened the door and saw Garry coming out of his room. I could hear that Sunny was crying behind the closed door. He never saw me, and he went straightaway to the bathroom.

Uncle Paul was just sitting in the lounge, facing the television. Like what he did before, he never stopped Garry from upbraiding his daughter. Uncle let his son Garry hurt the poor child. At all times, I thought it would be the parents' control of how they would run their home. However, this house was different from the other. I could understand that if you were older, you have the rights to command the younger ones.

"Hi, uncle", I said.

"What are you doing, Kevin? You are just standing there the whole time?" He questioned me with an interrogative face.

"Yes, uncle, I even saw Garry coming out from his room. By the way, is your daughter okay?" I asked.

"She's fine, but acting so poor. You know, brother and sister relationship", he replied.

I immediately went to my room and lay down without sorting out myself. I didn't have sufficient vigour to do it so. I lay my back flat, closed my eyes and took a nap. Fortunate enough, the nightmare never visited me.

■■

After dozing, I headed off to the bathroom, and cleaned my body. I wanted to make something to eat, but my food was running low. I went outside to buy small groceries to cook myself a meal. While walking back home, I saw the same car that my auntie and uncle's visitors were using, and the same car that dropped off my auntie many months ago.

My aunt stepped out of the car, and gave the old man a heated kiss, the same good-looking visitor that was lasciviously looking at her. Such scene caused me a sense of disquietude. My mind was troubled, and my body was shaken up. I didn't know what or how to think.

"My auntie will not do such a disreputable thing", I whispered.

As she opened the door, I tried to soothe myself, and called her name. She looked at me, and smiled. My auntie Lorette showed not one bit of disturbance.

"Hi Kevin, what are you doing there?" Auntie Lorette asked.

"I bought something to eat, auntie," I responded.

I had the desire in my heart to ask auntie Lorette concerning what I saw, but my mouth seemed to be sealed for an unknown reason. Inside their house, my aunt gave uncle Paul a warm hug. I prepared my food and reached their conversation. I perceived nothing but laughter between them.

"I'm off my head", telling myself.

I was not sure about what I saw. All I was sure about was that my uncle and auntie have been together for a long time, and love each other. She will not put her family in a scandalous situation, as well as my uncle.

Later that night, I moved towards my resting place, and put my imagination at ease. I stopped reasoning, and let my eyes close on their own good time.

"May this night be longer than a day, so I can prolong my rest."

I felt nothing but calmness.

■■■

"Kevin, are you awake", I heard my uncle knocking on my door.

It was already late. I overlooked at the time, and I had a long-lasting rest. I got up swiftly and opened the door.

"I'm really sorry, uncle; I'll be ready in a minute", I muttered.

"No hurry. I just wanted to talk to you", he despondently responded.

Chapter 8: Climbing Up

"Can I come in?" There's a courteous voice outside of the room- a voice coming from a man.

"Come in," I said in return.

It was a different person with a fantastic look- a classy, angular visage. The man was young and pleasant. He's wearing identical white clothes, just like the young lady who assisted me previously. He did not speak much.

He held my hand, and guided me to the bathroom. I only sensed helplessness within me. He gave me a bath like a new-born child. Still, I did't know what happened. I had no idea, no image, and no thought about me.

When everything was done, he laid me down on my bed, and asked me if I need anything.

"Please pass the book", the last thing I requested.

"The only way to finish things is by doing it."

It was a bright and sunny afternoon, and I tried to get lunch for myself. I was in a rush because I wanted to have more sales. I joined my old friend, John, and we consumed our food as fast as we could. We were both working in a car dealership as salesmen.

The air that I'm breathing caused my life. I must say that it has never been easy for me. However, I am lucky enough to meet a beautiful woman who supported me to improve my condition.

I met Rebecca when I was working as a call centre agent. She stunned the crowd with her gentleness, and I cannot explain how beautiful Rebecca is. No words can demonstrate her existence on earth.

Our heart-pondering days are still fresh in my memory, just like yesterday.

At the end of a long-day work, I would pick her up from the workplace, and drop her off at her house day by day. It became our routine.

Above all, I always had time to enjoy my own. After all of the sacrifices and bone-breaking duties that I'd been through, I think it's time for me to indulge myself.

I made a lot of deal, and got paid with a generous amount of money; it helped me elevate my position, and gave me more confidence. Even so, I knew that my life would not be going to end on this. I knew in my heart that I would never stay as a salesman for the rest of my life. I can be more than this.

Every day, I was waking up happily looking at my car parked in front of my house. It might not be the most expensive car, but it was the first.

The recollections of my mortifying story were still alive in my head while staring at my vehicle; they did give me hope for tomorrow.

I am so grateful that I didn't need to beg for a job and earn so little. I am glad that I had my own car and didn't need to wake up early in the morning just to take a taxi in a crowded place to reach work without getting late. I sweated blood, working day and night, and now slowly getting the sweet prize.

Before my job as a salesman, and call centre earning commission, I did not only one, but many strenuous jobs.

I was working under the sun as a construction worker, performing inside of the filthiest room as a cleaner, moving as fast as a machine as a packer, and far worst.

Each experience that I survived, my mum was always with me in every step that I chose. She's always there every time I needed her. She never let me down, not only in finding a job but also in my personal life.

I remember how I got involve in one of the most dishonourable issues that could ever happen to a man. I was accused of rape a long time ago. I went to a year-end party at my workplace. One lady filed a charge against me for a statutory offence, but there's no way on earth that I could do such a malicious thing. I believe they lay blame on me because I was the only one who could seemingly do it. The way that I present myself didn't show any creditable attribute. My looks and way of dressing up introduced me as a culprit. I was an unfortunate cleaner, as well as down and out.

I went to the smoking area to take my cigarette, and I saw the lady drunk and almost unclothed, shedding tears. I screamed for help, and that's it. Unexpectedly, I was the one being blamed, yet I didn't have disappointment helping her. My job ended as a janitor; the judgement in people's eyes while spending some time in jail for a crime I never did were not considered enough to give up.

I wasted my weeks in jail, while mum was helping me to clear my name. We didn't have funds to pay someone to defend me. No credible lawyers, no power, nor connection, but even so, I was set free.

I didn't know what happened to the woman who made the accusation. From my perspective, she couldn't identify who tried to harass her being so intoxicated with alcohol, so she blamed me to ease the pain, or maybe embarrassment. However, I was praying that one day she'd get the justice that she deserves.

Until now, I hold that incident closely in my hand. It serves as a lesson that there's no safe place elsewhere for each one of us. There are only two things in this world; it's either keep yourself safe, or put yourself in danger.

Only heaven was the witness how mum helped me, and I am glad.

I had a nice warm bath, dressed myself up neatly, and sipped a cup of hot chocolate milk before going to work. I started driving at six in the morning, and I fetched Rebecca; both of us went to our different places.

I persuade clients to buy cars; just like before, I was trying to win their hearts, and earn percentage amongst others. I got criticism, and was treated as a competitor by all and sundry, aside from John.

We're really good friends. John and I started our closeness when we were working as a packer, alongside Harold. We were separating all fresh products from rotten ones. The three of us had a great time of our youth despite of uneasy task. In such a short time, the reality of life separated us; no one wanted to stay where we were, and for so many years, we were lost in touch. Way back in time, I still consider that I'm favoured enough to work with my friend, John, once again. We've been asking each other about what happened to Harold, but we got no answer from both of us.

I finished my job early, and I picked up Rebecca from her place. We spoke about our day, and we began talking about having another job.

"You think I can find another work, Rebecca?" I asked.

She looked at me, astounded.

"You can. You are good in sales. Try to think about selling other things more than cars."

I could not hide my happiness. She has always been supportive no matter what. She gave me the idea of doing my next step, and I was sure that it was the right time for me to do new things. I had a good job, but I could be better.

We reached Rebecca's house, and I gave her a warm and loving hug. Afterwards, I continued driving back home, thinking about what kind of career I have to look for.

Soon, as I entered my house, I went straightaway into my room, and lay my back. I was thankful for every single thing that I have. I might not have the fanciest or expensive material things, but I can afford to take care of myself and mum. I can afford to treat myself and live in a comfortable environment. Most importantly, my nightmares diminished, and the monster departed from my senses.

I slept in calmness. The surroundings were full of peace.

■■

The first thing that I did in the morning was to look for an employer that was hiring a salesman based on my experience. It was the end of the week, so I had all the time to search for a company.

I used my whole weekend looking and hunting. In the end, I ended up in a company that sells properties. It's about the sales; I took a chance to send my curriculum vitae. Now, I have to wait for their response within a week.

■■

Early in the morning, I received an email from the firm where I sent my qualifications. My heart was filled with happiness when they gave me a chance to go to their office, and do a job interview.

I went to my work, and did my everyday performance. Just before I went home, I asked our sales manager that I would not be around the next day, and gladly, he allowed me.

My emotions filled up with thrill. I told everything to Rebecca on the way home, and she was amazed about it. I phoned mum, and told her the news, and I could hear the excitement in her voice. I was truly blessed, indeed.

∎∎

I got up early, and fixed up. I was nervous while getting ready for my interview, but I had to do it; I had to make it. I drove to the address where the building is located. I spoke to the receptionist, and she showed me the way up. My feet were shaking, and my hands were cold and sweating.

"Mr Kevin."

It was my turn; they called my name. I sat in front of the older woman. She looked at my curriculum vitae and asked questions about my experience. I was sure that I answered it correctly with confidence.

"You will work under supervision until you get your own qualifications in real estate. Don't worry, it will not take long", said the woman.

There was no explanation of how happy I was; I started from scratch, I never had good academic grades or any connections to anyone, but I felt the sensation of blessing. It might be a small thing for others, yet it was huge for me.

I gave my formal resignation letter to our principal dealer, and they approved it thereafter.

My employer wanted to keep me, but I made my decision. I wanted to do and try something new. Whatever the consequences are, I just have to embrace all of them. Later on, they allowed me to exit immediately.

I started my work under supervision, as discussed. No job is easy, not only for me but for every person who tried so hard to attain something. You have to put more labour to get what you want, and in the end, you will finally taste the fruits of your efforts. I have to learn all of their strategies in selling residential, commercial and industrial properties.

For a couple of months, I collected only the basic salary. I have to wait for my certificate to proceed with selling and marketing properties.

It was not easy. I am not an academic type of person. I never liked studying back then, but I tried my very best to pass the examination. And, after all the diligence, I eventually met all the requirements that the industry needed. I can now make sales. At this time, I am accredited to a real estate profession.

I started to do sales and dealt with so many people. I used my skills to win them over. I could not say that it is not a difficult job. It was heavy at first, but I always knew that I could make things happen, and I did. I sold my first estate in the residential area; I made a generous amount of commission. I sold second, third and so on.

I gained good and valuable things through my hard work. I could do things for me, mum and others. I had a humble and painful beginning. I started from scratch, and now I can do more, just like how I imagined myself- the beautiful result of dreaming big in life.

I treated my mum to a fancy dinner with Rebecca. I bought mum appliances, and gave her own extra money besides the monthly maintenance for the household. I also considered celebrating with my colleagues who supported me and believed in me throughout my journey. We drank a fine whiskey as a representation of success. It was my way of saying thank you to them. Aside from that, I never thought nor invited other people whom I never trust. Not one moment that they believed me. They should compare me to themselves and others. I kept everything away, even my achievements, from the people who could definitely pull me down. It's either a stranger, or even my own flesh and blood.

Nonetheless, I didn't stop putting in an effort. I didn't want to stop after selling my first property and another. I continued doing many things for mum and me. On top of that, I wanted to build a future with the woman I love; I wanted to create a family with Rebecca.

I am longing to start my dream without pain or torments.

Chapter 9: Triumph

As I was driving past Umhlanga Ridge going back home, all the huge billboards were noticeable. It was covering the side of the bridge. I saw an advertisement for a man who is familiar to me. It was Anthony. He was marketing his business. He still owns his investment company.

For so many years, Anthony and I never had communication. The reminiscences of yesterday were cloudless. He unmistakably shut us off in his house many years ago, showing an overt act of aggression. Anthony failed to think that I am his brother and mum will always be his mother at that time. He didn't scruple to ask us to withdraw from him. I guess, it happens on most bloodlines; there's always a rivalry.

I reached home late and exhausted, but much better because I didn't have to prepare a meal for myself every night. I would always eat with Rebecca after hours.

I washed and relaxed on my soft fleecy bed. I was waiting for another day of functioning.

My quiet sleep got disturbed when the alarm on my phone went on.

I slowly opened my eyes, and right away, went to bathroom. Subsequently, I put on my white-collar long-sleeved shirt, and paired it with black pants and a shiny opera pump, completely different from what I was. I didn't look like a vagrant anymore.

Before leaving the house, I made a nice omelette with a hot strong black coffee for breakfast. I finished my food quickly; I didn't want to be late for work.

I started walking far distance going to work back then. I bought my first white Fortuner car, and at this moment, I'm driving my second vehicle. A brand that I've been dreaming of for so long. I now owned a Mercedes Benz. I am joyful driving my dream car heading to work.

I arrived at my job on time, and kept moving. I was in great shock when I saw my long-lost friend, Harold. He worked in the same company, but in different designated area. Just before I left my job in a dealership, John and I have thought about where Harold is. Now, he's right in front of me. Destiny really showed me light and gave me a lot of blessings for these past years. I am thankful.

We talked and laughed once again- both of us remembering our youth. Time flew so fast to everyone. He already has his own family.

I invited him to see me one of these days, and he did. He phoned me, and we had a good time at Whalebone Pier in Umhlanga. We walked the whole afternoon at the pier, talked about my job with John, and decided to sit on a bench facing the sunset.

While looking at a beautiful view, I noticed a pile of newspaper on the side.

"My uncle owns this newspaper business, and I used to work there." I started.

"Your relatives must be rich", he said.

"And kind-hearted", I continued.

He surprisingly looked at me, and asked me what my relatives did to me when I was working for them. He demanded an explanation for the things I've said. Harold wanted to know what made my relatives kind-hearted.

"The rich will always benefit at the end, where we thought it was an act of kindness."

I was staggered by my friend's words. He was sure that it was not an act of kindness, but purely business. It was trading between them and me.

I told him that I have to pay for my room, my own groceries, and there's a time that I had to pay for lights and water with my small salary.

"I'm not their responsibility, Harold. I don't have regrets doing it", I responded.

"It is up to you, Kevin. But don't ever think that it was a deed of goodwill. One day you'll understand", the last words that came from him before we departed from each other.

I don't know when we will be seeing each other again. However, I wish that one day, the three of us can spend time as young boys again.

■■■

Years passed by, and I was at the age of thirty-three. I could say that I actually progressed in life.

I started working at the age of seventeen, and stayed with my uncle at the age of twenty-three. Until one day, I had to go back home to mum. My own uncle asked me to leave their home. I felt devastated at that moment when he knocked on my room, while I was rushing to get out of bed because I thought I was late to work. But I never knew that it was my last day working for them. I didn't have any idea why I had to go. He never gave me the reason; I felt abandoned at that time. I travelled at that the same day from Sandton, Johannesburg, to Phoenix, Durban.

At least today, I understand why it happened to me. If my uncle never required me to go, I might still be working for them, and earning less for the rest of my life. I'm still grateful for what they did.

While working for four years in the real estate profession, I also managed to invest my income from my commissions in purchasing properties. I started in a small investment, buying and selling houses. My portfolio became huge, until now.

Rebecca and I decided to get married in the warm and lovely month of August, 1986, and started to have a family. We have been together for two years, and seeking to have our own child.

My mum is truly happy about my success; how I wish that everyone can be happy for me, like my mum. I can never demand for more things in life; I know that I am fortunate enough.

I do more businesses other than investing in properties. I injected capital in a start-up company for ownership and market share in those entities.

My proudest moment is when I partnered with three prominent business people. We applied for government finance to purchase fifty luxury liners and double-decker coach buses that arrived on a ship from the country of Brazil that crane offloaded.

We renovated a space at Durban station, and employed the most stunning and well-groomed staff to accommodate travellers who wanted to be transported to major cities in South Africa like Cape Town, Port Elizabeth, and more.

Within three years, we made significant profits, and our loans were settled. I left my job as a real estate agent, and focused on my own realm.

I met a lot of different people who do different dealings. I closed a lot of deals, and I made trades in different firms and organisations. I became more confident about myself. The more successful I become, the more optimistic I am as a person.

While drinking a hot cup of coffee, facing the breath-taking ocean view of my house located in Zimbali, I remember all the fulfilments that I had.

I travelled the world with my wife. We went to Cambodia, Thailand, Vietnam, Singapore, Egypt, and other European Countries. Both of us experienced different cultures, seeing different faces, and embracing distance and diversity.

I became the apple of the eye of many. My assets landed on the sight of hundreds of thousands of people. My title became known all over.

At last, I don't need to live in somebody else's house because I already have my own. I don't have to experience mockery from other people, and I don't have to worry about tomorrow. My life is secured by now.

My bank balance grew significantly, a considerable amount of money that can sustain my family and me for the rest of my life. As I always said since I was young, "I am more than this." And now, I proved it not only to everyone who never believed my capability, but also to myself. I established my own worth.

I never had good academic grades, wealthy parents, or a golden spoon in my mouth, yet I succeed. As I close my eyes every night, my heart only feels contentment with all of the things that I achieved in life.

The greatest thing is that my nightmare of youth never revisited me. The monster lurking into the shadows under my bed was finally diminished. All I can see is hope, and the future for tomorrow. I eventually sprouted, after so long, to a strong fine man.

As soon as I finished my coffee, I stopped reminiscing about my accomplishments. I heard my phone ringing, and it was from an unknown caller.

"Hi Kevin, it's me", a soft-spoken voice from the other line.

Chapter 10: Harmony between Two

"Mum, help", I howled and called mum's name in my dream. I woke up in so much fear, and the nervousness awakened my helpless body. I could feel the perspiration on my skin; it was flowing from my head down to my neck and my entire body. The bed was wet and immersed in liquid. I was bathing with my own sweat.

I had a horrid dream. My head hit the ground; my blood spilled all over the floor. There was an unclear face standing beside me, but not doing anything. Every part of me trembled, and all I did was to call my mother.

I could feel the hurt of my dream. Although I was already awake, the emotion was exceedingly strong and heavy. The sharp pain was running inside my head, circulating all over. I knew to myself that I could not be overcome this.

The room was swallowed by twilight when suddenly the lights switched on.

"Are you awake? It's time for your medicine now."

It was the man wearing the same charming smile, the man that I don't like. He was still wearing his reading glasses, and his long white coat with the black long-sleeved polo inside.

"You must be the medic here", I asked.

"You finally identified; let's see how far can you remember." He responded.

He gave me the same medicine that that was given to me by the young lady. Until now, I don't like the aura of this man. He is my doctor, but I wanted him to be around nowhere close to me. I'd rather see the face of the man who gave bath to me an hour ago than to see the face of this doctor. I just cannot adore him.

"Where are the people who aided me before?" I asked him once again.

"You mean the nurses? Their shift is over. You'll see them tomorrow," and he went away.

I can't sleep anymore. My tranquillity was disturbed. The only thing that I can do is read the book beside me.

"The worst things come in one of the best moments of our time."

I purchased a plane ticket flying from Durban to Cape Town. I left my wife at home because of her job, and asked her to wait for me 'til I come back. I got ready and drove to the nearest airport from where I'm living.

After almost two and a half hours of flight, I managed to book into my hotel. I reserved a room right in front of a fantastic view of Camps Bay.

I sat on the balcony of my unit, and enjoyed the scenery. The highly pleasing red wine complementing the satisfying medium-well rib-eye steak with mushroom sauce was presented to me. I savoured every single taste that I had, and my whole day was delighted.

Thereafter, I phoned my wife as I'm always doing every time I'm out of her sight. I wanted to make her feel that both of us are safe. We exchanged loving and warm conversation, and decided to meet our separate beds for this cold evening.

Tiredness overcame me, and I quickly fell into a deep sleep.

■■

The morning rose, and I was almost awakened. I opened the faucet and immersed myself into a bathtub. The warm steaming water soothed every single part of my body. I submerged for one hour, and finally stood.

The soft towel made my skin dry in every part. I gave my face a glimpse, and I noticed the difference between before and now. I look younger and happier today. Eventually, I put my white golfer shirt and skinny jeans pants on me- a more casual look.

I went down to see the places throughout. While looking around, one restaurant caught my eye. I sat and asked the server to show me their menu. The meal listed were all appealing to me. I decided to order Portuguese chicken, and spicy, savoury prawn- undeniably heavy food for breakfast.

"I am waiting for someone. I want you to serve it hot and put extra sauce on it," I requested.

At that exact moment, I couldn't wait for him to come. My feet sweated under, and my entire body could not be still. I released a long wind coming from inside of me, a long breath out of anticipation.

"Kevin, I am here", with a tone of excitement.

Now, I heard it once again, the soft and melodic voice of my brother. He looks exactly the same after sixteen years of loss of sight. Anthony still carried his brown angelic eye, but his usual brunette hair is now tinted with black. I could see long years of a bygone age for both of us.

I gave him my hand as a greeting. I could not hug him. The past moment between us is still lying on me. I am not wrathful, but not peaceful either.

"Please sit here", I kindly demanded.

"You look different; it's a great thing", the first compliment that came from him.

I replied and said, "Who would ever expect?"

It was a cold response from me. I just wanted to say it for no apparent reason. I never had a grudge against Anthony, but I was also not pleased. Yet, I am happy. He thought of me like nothing and helpless almost two decades ago, and at this present time, I ended up proving my worth. I am not useless as a person, neither weak.

We talked for a short time when our food finally arrived. The prawn and chicken were truly mouth-watering. They were presented to me the way I wanted them.

I took my first bite, and fell in love with the taste. It was divine. The prawns were nicely marinated to their smooth, spicy sauce, and the chicken was tender and almost melting in my mouth.

My brother and I started talking to each other. He asked how's my life since then. I believe that it was a long question to be answered.

"Eighteen years of tales can never be told in one seating, I think?"

"Then tell me the recent story", enquired Anthony.

I only opened my lips about being married for two years, and planning to have a child. I never spoke about my business; I never made him aware of it. I guess, he didn't have to know.

Time passed by, and we finished the meal in front of us. In the end, I was delighted that my brother was standing still right in my face, alive and existing.

Suddenly he asked me in a curious pitch, "How long are you planning to stay here in Cape Town."

"I will fly back to Durban in two days. My wife is waiting for me."

Anthony asked me if I could meet him tomorrow night. He wanted us to have a drink. First, I was doubtful, and wanted to say no. I have a different view in my own life, particularly having drinks with somebody. I'd rather enjoy the night alone than drinking anywhere else without my wife. Rebecca always wanted to be beside me as always, and I adore it.

"It will be short. I want to talk to you, sincerely." He added.

We left each other, and went to our separate places. I've been thinking about my brother the whole night. I don't know if I must spend time with him or not. My head says that it is not my responsibility to be by him, but my emotions say differently. Maybe, it is the right time for us.

"I will go", the last words that I said before going to sleep.

■■■

Another period was wasted, and the day had passed. I was patiently waiting for the sun to go down. Anthony and I were going to have some drinks. We set time on seven at night.

In the moment of an hour, I took out my formal suit. I put my tuxedo on me, and paired it with an elegant leather shoe. I sprayed my best-loved perfume that disperses from one end to another. The spicy smell blended perfectly into the wind. As I was walking by, I could scent my own body. It made me feel more self-assertive.

I went to the place where Anthony set our meeting. It was a bar. I opened the door and used my eyes to identify him- plenty of people having fun from side to side. Later on, I heard him calling me and guided me to the gentleman's lounge.

"Kevin, these are my friends", introducing me to his two mates.

The earth swallowed me in disbelief, thinking that it would only be me and him, but it was my mistake. He invited his own friends. Faces that I do not know.

Four of us requested a drink, and we decided to have an expensive range of whiskey. I was shocked when Anthony's two friends asked me about my business and investments.

"How come all of you knew about my way of living," I asked out of curiosity.

"It is all over. It was on advertisements and social media," they answered.

I thought it would be better for my brother not to know everything about me, but I was wrong. He already knew. Many of them knew.

Like I said just before I went to this place.

"My name became the apple of the eye of many, my assets landed on the sight of hundreds of thousands of people, and my title became known all over."

I talked about the buses from Brazil that were now moving all over and producing abounding profit. I also shared information about my real estate investment.

After I told them about my investment, they gave me one question, "So you follow your brother's path?"

"No, I follow my own", I confidently responded.

After a brief moment talking about my life, the ambience of the place where I was sitting shift to another topic immediately. They started speaking about their own matters in life, and gradually, everything became light to each of us. The intimidating feeling that I felt starting to fade. We became more open, and the humour slowly opened up.

While in the middle of enjoyment, Anthony requested in front of everyone if I could come with him for a short minute, and I did follow him on his way. We tried to look for a less loud place, and we found one. He looked straight into my eyes. His eyes were saying something- a message of saying sorry. A statement that you could see and sense, but you would never hear.

Then I started to speak, "I am not mad at you. You don't have to apologise."

He just looked at me and never say anything. He was like a doll without a voice or sound. Nonetheless, he replied differently, reply that I never expected. Anthony gave me a tight hug, a hug for a long-abandoned brother. To be honest, I didn't know what to feel at that time. My emotion and logic were badly mixing together.

My head says that he is standing right in front of me because I am no longer a child; I am no longer hopeless. However, my emotions changed it all. My heart believes that he wanted to be with us. He is now the Anthony that mum once knew, the son that mum was so proud about.

Beyond everything, he is still my flesh and blood. He is my brother.

After spending personal time together about what happened between the two of us, we decided to go back to his friends, and continued our drinks. My head started to ache, and the alcohol was affecting my body. I felt that soon enough, I would be intoxicated.

As the hours continuously ran, I could not deny that I enjoyed the night spent with them. We drank the best liquors, and laughed at each other. All of us had so much liveliness. Anthony's friends were not the type of persons who were hard to spend boredom with. All of them were having fun, until one gentleman opened up about something, "I wish that Carl is spending time with us right now."

I stopped for a moment and questioned Anthony who and what happened to Carl. He nodded his head, saying that he didn't have any idea, and I never even got one answer.

Chapter 11: Where It All Started

"This will not gonna work for the both of us." Rebecca said.

Her tears were overflowing, and her eyes were full of pain. She wanted to leave me after five years of marriage, and shockingly, I felt the same way.

The fights between her and me became more aggressive day by day. We spent most of the time with our friends, socialising and clubbing every night. We are not the same couple that we used to be. We were not like this, but here we are, thinking where destiny may take us- a completely different path.

Rebecca would go with her friends to drink, and come home late. I tried to check who were going along with her, but every day, different faces.

Each man will think and asked the same way that I looked at our situation, "What happened to us?"

We carried on doing our lives separately. Rebecca and I might be sleeping on the same roof, yet we are no longer together. Our heated love departed from each other.

■■■

One typical day, when I was in the middle of a meeting with our fellow investor, getting updates, the compliance team was giving us information on how our transportation company has been doing. The meeting started very well, as always. The accountants explained financial reports, and told us that the business has been healthy for the past months. The project manager showed the company's positive growth, while the Human Resources wanted to present one unpleasant news.

Just before the Human Resources team started to tell everything, the secretary came inside the room with five drug enforcement authorities. They told us that two of our passengers were transporting a massive amount of drugs with the street value of eight million Rands using our luxury liners. All the investors, including me, denied the allegation when they asked if we were aware or involved in such deeds. Based on the authorities' story, one unknown caller warned them that drugs were stored inside the bus going to Johannesburg, and the officials confirmed it. The drugs were hidden in the luggage bag right inside the compartment. The two passengers are now facing a criminal charge of drug trafficking.

"This will affect our name", one investor spoke.

And one person in HR replied, "Positively or negatively."

After a long and exhausting meeting, I immediately went home to rest. I was still thinking about how the news would affect our business, when I saw my wife Rebecca, drunk. She talked to me terribly bad.

"How did the meeting go?" Rebecca asked.
"How many women have you slept with?" She added.

I never responded to her. I just looked at my wife from top to bottom. The meeting was a mess, just like her. Rebecca continuously drank, and finished all the bottles. I was not impressed with what am I seeing right now. Rebecca was in big trouble, and I couldn't help her. She was lying on the couch, and fell asleep.

A previous hour had passed, and I still couldn't figure out what I am going to do. My head was spinning, causing it to ache terribly. I was thinking about our transportation company, and how we are going to fix it. But I am also stuck with my wife's behaviour. I don't know where to go.

I left her sleeping, and went out to unwind. I went alone in a bar, drinking with no one. I enjoy the night far from any stress. Time was so fast that I never realised that it was already late at night. I drove back home, and saw no one. My wife was not around. She left the house out of nowhere. I was not happy, neither mad. I just don't have something to feel about her. I could perceive that there was absolutely nothing left between us. The delightful moments of yesterday were just a memory slowly fading, and the light of our heart was now swallowed by gloom.

I lay down in my bed, and closed my eyes. The monster was touching my feet, wanting to pull me under. I screamed as loud as I can, and I woke up. The sun was already up. I felt like I never slept for the nigh; right after I closed my eyes, they opened up quickly, yet the time passed. I was exhausted. My body was restless, and I could not move. I stared at my ceiling, and talked to myself, "He came; my nightmare came back."

As I was thinking, I heard the sound of the door. I got up and checked who is inside the house. I saw Rebecca.

I was dismayed at how my wife dressed up for the night. She never dressed the way she is right now.

"Where have you been?" I asked.

"You, where have you been?" She never intended to answer me. Instead, she asked me the same question in a debatable tone.

I knew that if I am going to answer at this moment, we will just end up having an argument that can lead us to hurt each other. I closed my mouth, and let Rebecca do what she wanted.

Rebecca went to our room, and slept away.

I spend my whole day stressing about what is going on. I've been thinking about the business and my wife, and unfortunately, the nightmare of my youth added. My brain cannot take any problem, and I feel that the situations are unmanageable.

"It can break me sooner or later", I said to myself.

I'm walking from one end to another, and I don't know what to do. My feet cannot be still in one place when my phone rings from the office.

They set another conference for the day, and each of us needs to be there. I fixed myself and went there at the exact time as discussed with me.

The meeting was about how we would shift the incident that happened on our transportation company into a positive effect, rather than negative.

We ended up agreeing that the publicity of our business name can affect us in a good way. The other investor shared the idea that we can release an article about how our transportation company helped the authorities catch the drug traffickers. It was a good idea that all we need to do is to hire a newspaper and media company that can release the story in the eyes of the public.

I offered everyone that I will be taking responsibility for looking for people that can make our story known and highlighted.

All of them went home, and I stayed in the office for a while. I contacted someone who can help us. I tried to reach my relatives, hoping that they will answer. The phone rings in one of the departments of my uncle Paul's newspaper business.

At least this day has some good news. They answered my phone call, and I demanded if I can speak to the owner. I made the secretary aware that I am the owner's nephew.

The secretary hand over the phone.

"Hello, how are you, Kevin." It was an elderly voice of a man. My uncle Paul faces the life of being old, I guess. The tone of his voice says it all.

I told Paul my story and made him knowledgeable about my life as well as my wealth. At last, he finally recognised. He told me that he never expected that it is me who runs the investment and transportation company. He was astonished.

I talked to him over the phone and told him every single detail that needs to publish. First, he was second-guessing about my idea. He was very hesitant, and there's a lot of question inside of him.

"See it as a business and not emotion", I said.

I offered him a sufficient amount of money, and I added more. He accepted it at the end, and promised our business' positive views would call the individuals' attention before the roosters crow.

My heavy chest became light, and I breathed out the stress once again. I am looking for a good and favourable outcome. I got each one on the phone and reported that our good tale would be published tomorrow morning. I am happy, so everyone is.

■■■

Morning has awakened, and the story is all over. My uncle's newspaper company disclosed the incident about how the drugs were transported using our bus. It was portrayed just like how we wanted it. The paper represented our company as a moral and justifiable name. It was printed and written all over.

I contacted my uncle once again; I gave gratitude for what he did. He asked me if I could visit them in Johannesburg. They were still living in the same place where I stayed fifteen years ago. I was only twenty-three years old at that time. Now I am thirty-eight, running a good wealth and having a downfall on my five years of marriage. I knew from the start that we could not have it all; there are always consequences.

My uncle Paul added that Garry invited me to his engagement party for next week. Garry wanted me to meet his soon to be wife. I was doubtful, but I said yes to show respect and appreciation. Their company released our good name anyway.

I spoke to my wife, Rebecca, if she can come with me, but she showed no interest.

"You don't need me, and you never did", She said.

I was wondering where she was getting her irrational thoughts. I was so tired of her behaviour, but at the same time, I don't know what to do. Our marriage is going down the drain, and it is not a good thing if you are going to think deeply; we had a fantastic start: three years of a beautiful life with her, and two years of misery.

"What have we done, Rebecca?" I asked

She looked at me in despair and said, "Do you still want to show me as your wife for one last time?"

She went away and did her own things. I have no one to come with me, yet I have to go.

Weeks have gone by like a cloud of smoke in the air. I have to travel all alone to meet my relatives. I wanted someone to be by me. I dialled Anthony's number, and he answered. I asked him if he can come with me to meet our relatives.

"Paul's family? There is no way on earth I will spend time with them," He coldly answered.

He's been battling from the past; as far as I could remember, he never wanted Paul. He always hated that man. Anthony never agreed to an idea that uncle must be anywhere close to us. He did not want him to be around.

Since we met three years ago in Cape Town, I am grateful enough that my brother also started communicating with our mother. He barely talked to mum, but at least he is trying.

"I think it will be nice to see them again. A small family reunion, what do you think?" I said while trying to convince him.

"You're right. Maybe, this is the right time", Anthony added.

He accepted my request, and I bought a plane ticket right away. We booked a place to stay for a couple of days just before we landed.

Another day had passed, and Garry's engagement party is marked on my calendar. It is set today. Anthony and I dressed up in the best way, and we drove going to their place.

"How did you know this place?" Anthony enquired.

"I worked for them, and stayed for a year," I responded.

The driving is peaceful; however, it is not the same place I once remembered. The town is filled with mini shops, and people are scattered all over.

We stopped and finally arrived at my uncle's place. I cannot wait to meet them.

Everyone is there: Uncle Paul, Auntie Lorette, Willy, his wife Elaine, his daughter Nadia and Garry, especially with his fiancé Grace. Also, uncle and auntie's daughter Sunny is there. However, she is not Sunny anymore. Her pretty face is dimmed by sadness. Her age changed, but not everything about her. She was still the scared child that I met long years ago.

We talked about our lives, and how we are doing. Our relatives are still working in their company, and the business is going strong. They are all amazed when they found out about Anthony's life and mine. They never expected the impossible thing on us, but it happened. We worked for the things that we have right now.

The party started, and everyone's eye was focused on Garry's soon-to-be wife, Grace. She is highly stunning with her long-fitted dress.

Her bluish eyes are filled with happiness, and her perfect smile lights up the room. Each one of us is stunned by the couple in front of us. Who would never want Grace's beauty?

She never failed to astonish the crowd. Even my own brother, Anthony, just stares at her, full of amusement. While enjoying the party, I received a notification and looked at my phone. I saw a message from my attorney and mum. It says that I have to go back to Durban as quick as I can.

Chapter 12: Ultimate Betrayal

It is already twelve at night, but my eyes are wide-open. I resumed reading the book after the doctor went away. I closed the book, and placed it beside me. I wanted to open the window to get some fresh air, but just like before, my limbs are senseless. I cannot move my legs no matter how I tried.

My memories of the past do not want to visit me. I am stuck in this bed, not knowing what is going to happen tomorrow. My patience is running low, and I want to know what happened to me, but no one can give me the answer.

"I wanted to go back home", I said to myself.

I was in a devastating situation. I want to be home, but I don't have any idea where my place is. Not one person inside of this facility can help me more than myself.

"You will be fine", I convincingly said.

However, rest and the bed are not calling me yet. I hold the book once again, and slowly look at the chapter where I stopped.

Then I continue reading.

"The only boundaries we have is absolutely nothing."

"Is that true, Anthony?" I asked.

He looked at me, shocked, and his mouth, closed. He never responded for a minute 'til he asked me what was wrong.

I told Anthony everything about Rebecca, and how we ended up our marriage. Rebecca's last words were still wandering inside my head, saying, "Your brother is right about you." Until now, I don't know what she meant. I am aware that the only thing she can feel right now is anguish towards me, but I cannot imagine from my most profound thought that Rebecca would use my own brother. I wanted to ask her, but she never gave me a chance.

It's been a month since we separated from each other. My attorney sent me a message that Rebecca wanted to file a divorce and demanded half share of my wealth as we were married in a community of property, causing me to leave Anthony and the engagement party of Garry to go back home and sort out my own matters. My mum was dismayed towards us. She said that we were just wasting our time, and we were not young anymore. But who could actually stay in a marriage that has been dissolved for years. We never had a child nor reason to hold on. Rebecca was right. There's nothing left for the both of us.

I left Anthony in Johannesburg, and he went back to Durban alone after a couple of weeks. I invited him to come to my house and have some drinks with me, and he did. We faced the beautiful view in front of my house and exchanging thoughts about different things.

While we were in the middle of the conversation, I boldly confronted Anthony if he said horrible things to Rebecca about me, but he vehemently denied it. He looked at me straight into my eyes, telling me that he could never do such a thing. In the end, I believed my brother.

"He never loved you, Kevin", Anthony said.

I was doubtful about his statement. Rebecca was there when I was starting my life. I knew that she loved me; she did. It is just us who lost love and respect in our relationship.

But Anthony's confession shocked me and changed the way I looked at Rebecca. He told me that Rebecca never meant to give me a child- a child that we always wanted. Anthony said that there was a time that he and Rebecca were talking, and he was not impressed by her. Based on my brother's story, Rebecca didn't want to have a child, and was looking forward to her own career. She desired to build her own name.

It was a devastating feeling. I never expected Rebecca to see our future that way. We always wanted to have a big family- kids playing around and travelling around the world, but everything changed.

I really thought that it was the end of Anthony's story, but he added more that made my whole world tremble. I sensed that the soul inside of me left my body suddenly. There was a thunder that struck my spine that made me feel nothing.

"She was cheating", Anthony said.

I released a long breath, and responded, "How did you know, and why didn't you tell me?"

Anthony's confession broke me. From a man who never felt anything toward his ex-wife, not love, neither disappointment, I am now full of hatred.

Anthony explained to me that when he went to a club to enjoy, he saw Rebecca with another man, and he never got a chance to tell me those things because of what's been going on with me and my business. Anthony told me that he was aware that I cherished Rebecca so much that it could affect me in every single way, financially and emotionally.

All those times flashed on my head so quickly. There was a night when she was not around; she'd come home late and almost blind because of alcohol that led us to terrible arguments.

"No, she could never do such things. It must be her friend." I said.

"It is not just a friend, Kevin. There is more between them", he added.

I am speechless, and I don't have anything to say. Anthony apologised to me, and I accepted it. Instead of getting mad at him for telling me, I saw it as a gesture of care. He is correct. It would affect me. Besides, I also wanted to come out with my marriage, but I had been thinking about the years that Rebecca and I spent together. There was also a time that we had a lot of passion for each other, yet those memories cannot conceal the presence of misery to the awaiting future between us. One of us needs to make way.

After talking to Anthony, he told me that he was going back to Cape Town to oversee his business. After we met at one of the finest restaurants in Cape Town three years ago, he decided to move back to Durban.

He had a nice time spending with me here while continuing with his company for a good couple of years. But now, he needs to go.

Everything seems to be well on his side. I think we are meant to have the same destiny. We became successful on our own. However, we paid for the consequences. Our wives left us. Rebecca left me not so long ago, and Alexa left him, and took away his child. Another bittersweet life of us.

■■■

Another week passed. Anthony made me aware that he would depart and leave another three years of memory in Durban. He also spoke to mum about his departure, and separated their way.

Rebecca and I finally agreed on one thing- we both signed the divorce settlement. At least it was over. I sold our house, and bought a new one. I wanted to start a fresh and new life. I cannot live with the past, and I have to move forward. My business continuously grew, and I became more focused on myself. I learned what self-love is.

My life is going smoothly. I went from places to places, and enjoyed the things that I have. This time, I only have my mother. I am glad that my mum stopped asking me to get married and forcing me to start a new family. I am not ready, I guess. My clock might be running fast for other people who are looking at me, but not for a man who is happy where he is. I am contented to be alone for a while. Time will come that I'll think about having a family once again, but I am sure that it is not too soon. I am the holder of my own destiny.

Like I said, I move from one place to another. I went to Milan last month all alone. I also visited Pinacoteca di Brera, Italy's finest art museum; the place is gorgeous, yet

I have to go back to South Africa, the only place where my heart is.

I never spoke to Anthony for so many months, and I have been thinking to call him. While planning back home, I settled that I will be visiting him at his house. I landed at the airport, and immediately found his place, hoping that he is staying at his property situated at Clifton district in Cape Town. Anthony's home address is Camps Bay's sister neighbourhood, where I booked my hotel to meet him a long time ago- the place where we reconciled with each other.

Hours were gone, and I finally found Anthony's house. He lives in the most desirable area. The wave is uninterrupted, and the mountains are exceptionally spectacular. I am fortunate enough to reach his home at golden hour; I witnessed the beautiful sunset dimming the entire ocean.

I knocked on his door, and he was not the one who opened it. The one who is standing in front of me is very familiar. It is the face of a captivating and beautiful woman. It is Grace. Garry's soon to be wife.

"Please tell me that what I am thinking is not right, Anthony", I said.

He had not, for one moment, disagreed nor expressed any clarification about what I was thinking about him and Grace. It seemed like I don't deserve an explanation.

"Whatever you are thinking, it is right, Kevin", Anthony spoke.

I don't know what to say. I am not impressed, but overwhelmed with guilt.

My thoughts were right; Anthony and Grace are in a wrongful relationship. She will marry our cousin, yet my brother has the nerve and audacity to be with her unethically. I am traumatised. I never wanted to be in a situation wherein I have to tolerate any wrongdoings.

"What did the both of you do?" I asked in a displeased tone.

I looked deeply into all of the signs that my brother showed from the day he met Grace. It was the day of her own engagement party. The way he glared at Grace, and offered her a ride on his expensive sports car should have at least warned me that something was wrong. I should have forewarned him about the possible danger, and never condoned his desire. But I was also caught up in my own life.

I made them aware that I cannot swallow this kind of activity; therefore, I have to do something to stop this. However, Grace cried like a vulnerable child. She begged me not to tell anyone about their relationship, especially Garry.

She promised me that she would leave Garry as soon as possible. Grace said that she was no longer happy with our cousin, and found love and comfort in my brother. The way that her tears flowed can fill the floor.

"What did really happen?" I'm questioning myself in silence.

Grace and Anthony justified their behaviour. She told me that Garry was beating her up badly to the point that bruises and blood covered her whole body. Furthermore, Garry was constantly thrashing her across the head and shoulders. There was a time that Garry insisted on her and abused her. Based on Grace's story, she tried to leave him so many times, but he was threatening her. I can see her as a scared child victim.

I cannot dispute Grace's confession. I saw Garry's violent way of conduct when I lived with them long ago. I was there when he was hurting his own sister Sunny, a seven-year-old child.

I am a living witness of how he treated his sister, and there is not one moment that I did something to help the poor child. I cannot do anything, and even their father

Paul, my uncle, never stopped Garry's violence. They indeed raised a vicious child.

"I hope that you can feel my pain. If he found out, he will kill me," Grace said.

"We are not bad people, but we have to do terrible things", I responded.

Chapter 13: The Downfall

"Sir, someone wants to speak to you." My secretary knocked on my office saying that one unknown person in his mid-forties wanted to speak to me. However, I never talked to anyone, nor set an appointment. It is a busy week for me.

"Tell him to come back tomorrow", I said in return.

My life changed so tremendously since I decided to be all alone. I had a lot of time seeing myself from within. I spent time with my mum whenever I could, and lived only for a day. I thought, living all by myself will be fine; however, I still yearn for love. There is emptiness in my heart that no one can fulfil.

My house is no longer a home. It is nothing for me. I sleep and wake up doing the same thing repeatedly, 'til one day, I realised that it is becoming exhausting. I cannot leave like this.

I went to my workplace early in the morning, and saw a man standing in front of my office. He was tall and charming.

"Mr Kevin", the man spoke.

"How can I help you?" I responded.

He looked at me, and breathed deeply, saying, "I am Carl Lawrence, and I am looking for your brother, Anthony."

I asked him to come and sit with me. His story was unacceptable for me. I know in my heart that Anthony cannot bear to hurt someone. He can never plant pain into someone's heart. Yet, Carl's way of telling a tale was recognisably true. I could see in his eyes the pressure to find my brother.

He told me that many years ago, my brother asked him to sign a trust document that Anthony drew with an attorney, and without any hesitation, he signed it.

Everything went smoothly with both parties. They continued living as friends, 'til one day, my brother stopped the communication with him. He never had any idea why, but he never asked nor bothered Anthony. However, he found out that Anthony was using the trust to open up bank accounts and take loans from several financial service providers. According to Carl, he was so devastated. The banks were now sending letters to his home stating that it's either one of them must pay all the debts. The amount of money that my brother owed was unbearable, as well as the interest.

"How come that you have to pay for it?" I asked.

"The trust documents clearly state that both of us will be responsible for any financial obligations conducted under the trust", he replied.

I slowly felt disappointed to Anthony. I didn't know who would I believe, but there was proof in front of me; Anthony was accountable for this.

I could sense that Carl was truly displeased with this matter; all he wanted was to see my brother. I tried to phone Anthony in front of him, showing that I am not knowledgeable and cannot condone any of this act. But it seems like the gentleman sitting right next to me is unfortunate for we could not reach my brother; I contacted Anthony's number, but I got no answer.

Out of frustration, Carl asked me if we could have some drinks for the day, and I immediately agreed. I had a lot of things to do, but I didn't want to leave him hanging anywhere, and searching for the person who doesn't want to be found. An arduous task, I think.

Both of us went to the nearest bar, and shared a drink. I enjoyed talking and spending time with him. We talked about our personal lives, and sadly, both of us are divorced. I asked him what transpired, but he just smiled, and looked away. He never wanted to give me an answer.

As Carl got intoxicated because of the alcohol, he started talking about his relationship with my brother. He told me that he and Anthony were really good friends back then- inseparable, as they said. While he was telling me the story, my memories almost four years ago came back. I met Anthony in Cape Town, and socialised with his two friends who mentioned Carl's name. I remembered one of my brother's friend who was hoping that Carl was around to spend leisure time with them. And when I asked my brother what they were talking about, he never responded.

Now I can understand; it is clear to me. From that time, he stopped speaking to Carl because of this.

Carl's resentments were not yet done. Aside from the trust that he had signed, he also agreed that he'd be responsible for Anthony's mortgage. Carl signed trust documents and suretyship for my brother's mortgage loan worth millions of Rands.

He told me that Anthony requested him to validate the suretyship one day, and he did, with a promise of financial rewards in return. Carl treated Anthony like a brother, and trusted him so much, but now, the friend that once he treated like a family was nowhere to be seen.

I could not say a word of encouragement to Carl; I was not happy with Anthony's behaviour, but I still felt that I had to speak to him first, and clarify things. I know where he is, but I cannot tell Carl right away. I want to talk to my own brother first, and ask for insights and clarification.

"May I leave you for a while?" I asked Carl.

He nodded his head, and I walked away. I tried to dial Anthony's number, but he was not answering his phone. I dropped him a message saying that I wanted to talk to him urgently.

I went back to our table to continue my drink. I intendedly looked at Carl and his situation; he is truly in a mess right now, in different aspects: emotionally, financially, and mentally.

I kept on chatting with him, and he was just so drunk that he could answer everything that would be asked to him, even his bank account. I enquired about his way of living, and he told me that he was earning sufficiently to provide for his needs and wants. He worked as a chartered accountant.

Carl smirked and said, "I once worked as a chartered accountant for your brother, don't you know that?"

I looked at him with full of questions in my mind. The tone of his voice was telling me that there was something more. He was not only a chartered accountant to my brother; it was undoubtedly more than that. I was so interested in his next sentences. I wanted to hear more things and open his mouth again. And he did.

Carl leaked more information about what he was doing for Anthony. I was already startled about the trust and suretyship, and Anthony's tax added up.

Carl told me that he was the one who was making two different financial statements for Anthony. They have balance sheets, income statements, and cash flow statements. They were Anthony's records of business activities and their financial performances.

"What does it even mean?" I asked for further explanation.

He replied to me, saying that the two financial statements were entirely different from each other. The first statement would show the company's negative performance, and those documents would be submitted to the revenue services. It showed the government that Anthony's business suffered from an undue loss in income and unexpected expenses that could not be avoided. The aim of it was to pay less to no tax at all. The other financial statement would show that the company was advancing on a year to year income growth favourable asset, with low liabilities and substantial cash flow. This statement was intended to entice the financial service providers that offer asset finance and equity loans. Anthony had been setting up shelves company, and applying the same scheme to swindle the financier. He's been doing it for a long time, based on Carl.

"It is fraudulent, Carl. And you know that?" I said.

He stared at me, and said, "I almost lost my job for your brother. Of course, I know that."

My feet started to shiver. I cannot imagine that my brother is doing this kind of unlawful deeds. If someone finds out, he will be in big trouble.

"That's how he is supporting his extravagant lifestyle. Fancy car, huge estates and his shiny things are all from money laundering. All fraud." Carl added.

The whole day passed for the both of us. Carl dozed for a couple of hours in the bar. While waiting for him to get up, I tried to reach for my brother once again, but there was no response.

Carl got up, and drove back home. Before he left me, he told me that I must contact him if I have any lead about my brother, and I gave him my words. We never set a date for our next meet up, but we told each other that we have to see our faces again. I agreed with him. I felt that I'd be needing to see him sooner.

I went back home, and no one was waiting for me. The reality hit me so hard, showing that I am alone in my big premise. My room can be compared to an empty soul. I cannot feel the same excitement when I am reaching my bed. My existence became more inconsolable. Nevertheless, Carl's story is somehow more important than living all by me.

I closed my eyes, stressing about the day that I had, and the story that I heard. I am here resting, waiting for another day to come. However, today, I am no longer alone in this house. There is someone inside my room looking at me, hoping that I'll be senseless so soon. I know that something is hiding in the shadow. I get up from my bed and put my bare feet on the chilly floor.

And from that moment, I know that it is right under my bed. There's an air wrapping my feet; there's entity breathing underneath.

I bend my two knees, and lower my upper body. My heart is beating rapidly. I cannot agree more that I am genuinely terrified.

I slowly put my head down to see what's there beneath the bed, but I immediately woke up, yowling, yet no one can hear my mourning. It was just a dream, another unpleasant night for me. I went to the shower, still frightened about last night. I had never slept; I think that I just closed my eyes and opened again in one snap. I dressed, made my food and started driving, going to meet my co-investor.

My secretary handed me over the two envelopes that she received this morning from the bank.

"I'll see this note after my meeting. Keep it for me," I said to my secretary.

Almost two hours passed by, and the meeting with my fellow businessmen was finally over. I completed some works and read all the updates about my businesses and investments. Time went by, and the darkness embraced the light once again. Before I went back home, I approached my secretary to show me the same letter that she tried to give me a while ago. I opened the first envelope, and found out that the bank sent a notice of indebtedness. The second one contained a letter stating the intention to foreclose and repossess the property.

My jaw nearly dropped while reading what is in front of me. I took my phone out of my pocket, and immediately dialled numbers. The call was left unanswered, so I left a short voice note.

"Please, phone me back. I want to see you as soon as possible."

I don't know what to do at this moment. I cannot think properly. All that I wanted to do was to reach my brother, and talk to him. I am not the only one who deserves an explanation. His friend is also waiting for him, longing for an acceptable reason.

Chapter 14: A Place of Nowhere

There's a sweet and gentle voice, calling me. I gradually opened my eyes and noticed from the window that the sun already rose for this day.

"How's your sleep?" It was her talking to me once again.

"The doctor visited me last night, and I was looking for you", I said in return.

"My shift was over last night," the lady said.

She guided me from my bed to the bathroom, and helped me clean myself. After that, the young lady placed me in front of the window.

"Foi. Such a simple yet elegant name", I said, while looking at the name tag pinned on her right chest.

"I will get your food and medicine. Please wait for me," she said in return.

After a while, breakfast was served on my table. They gave me bread toast with hot chocolate milk. Before I started to eat, I paused and stared at the scenery in front of me. I was still amazed, although I already saw this beautiful view. I am not sure what is going on with me. I cannot even remember what happened to my life, yet one thing is for sure, I adore the breath-taking view. There's an instinct, telling me that this is not the first time I fell in love with such scenic creation. It is me, a man who loves to witness impressive things.

I took a bite from my toast, and sipped the hot chocolate milk. It was not so special, but not bad either. I finished my food, and waited for the nurse to help me. I waited for them for a couple of minutes, and then, they came. The nurses took all the things that they put on my table. After that, they led me to my bed to rest; however, I am tired of doing this. I want to remember who I am, and why I am here. But all I can do is to lie down and waste my time waiting for someone to explain what I am doing here in this facility. A long patience is needed for this kind of situation, and I'm running low on it.

"Let me finish this book rather than stressing," I told myself while opening the book beside me.

"Some ears listen, and make stories fly."

Long months have squandered, and I took a long break from any problem around me. I am alone, living in my huge house, and taking care of myself. Last week, I got ill, and almost couldn't move. I never told mum because I didn't want her to get worried about me. I learned to aid myself, and at last, I felt much better.

My mum phoned me saying that I have to visit her house as quick as possible. After my divorce from Rebecca, I decided to sell our house, and I bought a new premise in Umhlanga, closer to mum. She is still living in Phoenix; my mum will never leave her place.

I travelled and reached mum within fifteen minutes. "Mum, open the door", I said.

The door opened immediately, but I got surprised when I saw that it was not my mother who opened the door. It was a very familiar face, yet I couldn't totally figure it out. I just looked at the man, stunned, asking myself who he is.

"Kevin, long time no see. This is me, your cousin, Mervin," he said.

Now, I remember my cousin who migrated to Australia with his sister, Addie, and their parents. The last time I saw my cousins was when I was twelve years old, and now, I am thirty-eight of age.

Mum and I welcomed all of them. Mum's brother, uncle Bob, and his wife, Louisa, were far from what I could remember. Maybe, we met when I was young, or maybe not. Mervin and Addie are recognisable, but unclear, because of the long years that we did not see each other. We all sat together, and my mother made food for us. They talked about their lives and they were very happy sharing their own story. I was just a listener who paid attention nicely.

After hearing all of them, they started to ask what I am up to. It is not my responsibility to tell people what I am doing in my life, so I made it clear and straightforward.

"I do several businesses and investments, nothing else," I said.

They insisted for more information about me, but I told them that it would be a long tale to tell, and made the rest of them aware that I was unwell and sick, so I couldn't assist them well. My relatives seemed to respect my choice, and we talked about something else.

"Does anyone have contact with Diana?" I asked.

I've been looking for her and trying to communicate with her, but I never got a chance. Not even one in our family knows where she is. For some reasons, I wanted to meet her. It was not clear why but I desire to talk to her again. Unexpectedly, her face was pictured in my memory; her words that night when we last saw each other was utterly clear.

Addie instantly answered and told me that she has Diana's contact number. I told her that I forgot my phone inside the car, and that I would get it to save Diana's details.

I went outside, and took my phone; just before I stepped inside the door, I heard my uncle Bob, saying, "Is Kevin really unwell? It looks like he's not sick at all."

"I don't know about his health. All I heard is that he is making a lot of money, and we don't know how, or if it's actually true," Mervin answered his dad.

I am so amazed how my relatives, who never saw me for so many years, can boldly talk behind my back. I pretended that I never heard anything, and handed over my phone to Addie. I kindly asked her to save Diana's number. I sat in front of them while waiting for mum's food. I pretended that I was listening, but my head and thoughts were flying all over. I was thinking about who could I trust this day. Not only strangers can talk or hurt you from your back, but our relatives can also easily do it to us. My brother whom I trusted so much, stabbed me at my back, and left me hanging. So, it would not be difficult for my relatives who are sitting in front of me to whisper.

Last month I talked to my ex-wife, Rebecca, to clarify and prove something. I asked about Anthony, and what my brother told her. She obviously didn't want to speak to me, but she told me everything in the end.

Rebecca told me that she was aware when I was with many women every time I went somewhere. She knew that I lost love for her. I spent my time going places to places, meeting people, going to clubs and drink with my brother and his friends, that I even forgot that I have a wife left at home and waiting for me. She reminded me that we had three wonderful years in our five years of marriage, and the last two years was a nightmare for both of us.

She refreshed my memory about the things that I had done for the past years. I separated myself from my wife, and no one must be blamed for this.

I remember the time when I came back home late and drunk. Since I reconciled with my brother, I spent much time outside my marriage, living like a single man. However, I never cheated on Rebecca. I forgot her for a day, but I never slept, or be with another woman.

I questioned Rebecca if she cheated on me, but she denied it. She told me that her behaviour reflected mine, but not one day that she thought about being unfaithful, contradicting what Anthony told me about her. She was not with any man, she didn't cheat on me, and I could see the sincerity in her eyes. Rebecca said to me that I badly changed, and I silently agreed with her. I was caught up in life outside my marriage, and now I cannot do anything about it.

"I remember the day that you asked me how many women I slept with. Who told you those things?" I asked Rebecca.

"Your brother, Anthony. He became my eyes every time I was not around. He told me everything. He cared about me more than you did," Rebecca said.

Carl's stories were right about my own brother. I phoned Carl when I received two letters from the bank, and when we met up for the second time, he told me everything, even his own marriage. He told me that Anthony influenced him, in a bad way, took him everywhere to meet different people, and spent most of the time to the club, partying than going home with his wife. He also told me that Anthony made up a story that he was cheating, which was why Carl's wife quitted on their long-running marriage.

Carl never lied about his stories. Anthony's fraudulent and wicked craft was truly undeniable. They were not just stories; my proof is in front of me- from Carl, to the bank letters, and now my ex-wife. They are the evidences of my brother's unscrupulous behaviour.

Carl and I experienced the same fate in the hands of Anthony.

I breathed heavily and readied myself to say goodbye to Rebecca when she asked, "Are they all true, Kevin?"

"Does it really matter, Rebecca? Will the truth change what happened between us?" I answered.

"I should have asked first. Am I right?" Rebecca asked.

I never gave her an answer, or told her that everything she heard from my brother was all lies. I am tired. All I have are regrets for not seeing people around me for who they really are. It is a disgrace for both of us for losing our love for each other because we never knew who we trusted.

"Who can you actually trust?" my last words for her before I departed.

■■■

"Kevin, I have been calling you for so many times," mum said.

I did not hear what mum have to say, nor listen to my relatives. I was still stuck, thinking and daydreaming about Carl and Rebecca's disclosures.

.

"Yes, mum, what's that," I said in return.

She asked me to set the table for all of us, and I did. We sat and ate what my mum made. They continued to ask questions, and talked, but I kept myself quiet. I felt like, for a long time, I never ate good food. I really enjoyed it, as well as everyone.

Mum asked them if they would stay in South Africa permanently, but they were not sure about it. Uncle Bob told us that he wanted to visit a beautiful place with his family first, and think about it later on. Aunt Louisa seemed happy staying in Australia with her children and grandchildren. Mervin and Addie have their own families already, unlike me. I cannot deny that I am longing to have a home once again.

"So, all of you still need to go back to Australia?" I asked.

"We have to. We left our family there for a short vacation," Addie replied.

I wanted to offer them my vacation home, but I was doubtful. I didn't want any further questions from them, so I kept my mouth closed, and never suggested, or said anything. Another day passed by, and the gloom is now all over. They were ready to go, but my mum stopped them and offered her house.

"We have three bedrooms here; all of you could stay. Don't worry about Kevin. He got his own place." Mum told uncle Bob

"That will be nice. Thank you so much, Anne", Uncle responded to mum.

Auntie Louisa told us that they would surely not stay for long. They would enjoy their home country's places, and attend one event where all of them are invited to.

"What event are you talking about, Auntie?" I asked out of curiosity.

"Are you and your mum not invited? It's a family event." She replied.

Chapter 15: The Suffering

"Are you sure you wanted to see me?", the voice said in the other line.

I took a deep breath and said, "Why are you hiding for so long?"

I never heard any explanation from the other side. All I got was a cold response saying that we would see our faces again. I dropped the phone call and sat with my comfortable chair, facing my window overlooking the beautiful ocean.

It is a nice and fine day to rest for me. I've been through a lot for a couple of months, and I couldn't handle more difficulty. Exactly five in the afternoon, and I'm holding a glass of wine in my right hand, patiently waiting for the sun to go down. I don't know what to think, or what to do. My source of living is doing great, but my personal life is far more different.

"I think I'm losing my mind", I whispered to myself. I feel alone all the time. I barely spend time with my friends, and, just lock myself in the four corners of my house.

I have just finished the glass of sweet red wine when suddenly my phone rang.

"Hi, Kevin. How's the weather in Durban. I'm doing great, but I am still stuck on this little mess, and I think I have to wipe it out on my own"

"I apologise, Carl. I wanted to help you, but I cannot", I said.

"You did a lot; at least we learned something from this." His last words before he cut the call.

He'd been experiencing this problem for a long time now. He tried to reach out to my brother, and asked for my help, but he failed so many times. Carl never got the help that he wanted. Anthony never lent his hand after all the mess that he made. I am too tired to put myself up with this kind of issue. I just want to let these things go.

Carl was forced to pay the bank as much as he could, but that was not enough to cover them all. Anthony took several loans from different financial providers that are under the trust. However, he needs to deal on an enormous debt, which is the property that owes millions of Rands, including the interest, and there's no other way that he can afford it. His name is crucial to him, so he needs to settle it as soon as possible.

I remembered when he told me that he got to speak to Anthony, but instead of talking to him, Carl was advised to contact my brother through his email address. For that moment, he felt like an ordinary worker of Anthony. Carl shared his feelings with me, and he was deeply disgusted about his experiences with my brother. He felt that he dug his own grave. Just imagine, signing trust and suretyship documents for a person you once relied on, and treated you like nobody, or evading you like a plague after using you is enough reason to destroy someone's life. Like what an old man said, "Don't put your faith on man." Always remember that there are two kinds of people out there. There's someone that once you give your hand for him to eat, he'll feel grateful, and he will take care of you. The second one is a kind of person that once you give your hand, he will also eat your arms, and will crave to swallow the whole you to the point that there will be nothing left.

It is the sad part of this world; sometimes, we don't know who's beside us and what he wants from us. We are doing good things for other people because that's what our heart desires, but it doesn't mean that we have to place ourselves at risk for the sake of their needs. Maybe there's a story behind why God put our brains first and, our hearts, the second; we have to use our intellect first, and the next one will be our emotion. By that time, we will definitely have wisdom within ourselves that can show us what is right, not just only for others, but also for us. It is like, "If I am going to give my hand, but he wants to take all of me, will it be reasonable? Will it also be healthy for me?"

It was the same thing that happened to Carl and me. We never used our wisdom. Instead, we used our hearts without our brains. In the end, we put ourselves at risk. We gave our hands to Anthony, but he wanted more.

It is not easy for me, as well as for Carl who suffered the most. He told me that the banks couldn't get Anthony, so they were going after him. Carl tried to phone and message Anthony, but he was only answering through emails.

As a real estate investor, I gave Carl advice that might help him about the property in Cape Town that was closed for repossession. I told him that he must sell the property that could cover the outstanding debt, including the interest that was not paid for many years. I gave him my words that I'll help him get a buyer for the property, but he needs to contact Anthony to sign the required documents, like the offer to purchase. He did it willingly, with a smile on his face. Carl, thanked me so much for looking for a buyer for him, yet he was not impressed by my brother. Anthony not only wanted to communicate through emails, but he also asked Anthony to drop the documents to be signed in his post box. I don't know if he is embarrassed by his acts, and can't face the man that he harmed, or he just has no care for anyone.

Carl is not the only one who suffered from Anthony's unlawfulness. Whatever Anthony did to him, was also done to me by my own brother. He never answered, or even thought to answer my phone calls. I couldn't even remember if I already made thousands of phone calls and voice notes to him, or not. My text messages got no response as well.

Exactly, as what I said, I have experienced everything. I also communicated to Anthony through his email. He has the intentions of evading me, and what he had done to me. I felt exhausted, but remained calm. I could still feel the anguish while writing to him. I badly wanted to say awful things, but I held my hand. I never said anything terrible, but I didn't get the answer that I wanted. I never signed for trust, but I stood as a surety for my brother. I could not imagine myself signing documents that could harm me. I am not sure if I signed the documents when I was drunk and blind because I cannot remember any of this.

What should I do now? All I can do is pick up the dirt that I made. This is what would happen when we trusted people too much, and forgot to think about what human nature could do. We are not holy, we are not righteous, and we can all do bad things.

I signed a suretyship for the loan that he took, and for one property that he purchased here in Durban. Sometimes, I was asking myself if a man could ever be witless like me. Who could actually think about these foolish things?

Since I got too tired of all of these, I paid the loan that he took that was worth millions. I looked for an investor who could pay for the property before it would be repossessed. I took money out of my pocket for the things that I had never seen. I am a businessman, and I am supposed to make money, and not spend it.

The investor saw the property as overpriced. If they would ask me the same, I would also not lie. I wanted someone to cover the debts, including the interest, for years, but I knew that it would be hard. In the end, I finished paying the outstanding balance. The worst part was, instead of him talking to me, Anthony ran away, and avoided me.

He ruined Carl's marriage like mine. He made us pay for the money that we never had and used. Anthony played on us on his palm. I thought he changed, but he didn't; it was the same Anthony back then. I should have reminded myself that he shut mum and me off when I was young. I should have told myself that he treated me like a worker, and not as a brother. I should have learned his ways that I noticed a long time ago when I was seventeen. He got used to taking advantage of people who are wealthy. He would not care for someone who didn't have anything to offer. I saw it, but I cleared it in my memory. I wished that I realised about all those things in the past, and did not fully trust him, but it's too late. Relationships were already broken, and the debts were already paid. I cannot turn back the time to correct things. I just have to deal with it.

He was raised with love by our mum, but he became greedy. His love for material things overpowered him. This must be the reason why his wife left him. I don't want to assume, but I guess, this was one of the reasons. Anthony is sick, and I will never deal with it. I have a life of my own. It's time for me to fix myself.

I settled everything in the banks, and my name was cleared. I don't want anything that has something to do with my brother. I can't even imagine his face after what he did to my life; he ruined me, so as some other people. But now, I'm sitting in my house, all alone, and losing my mind. Mum would not want this to happen, but I've been thinking not to communicate to Anthony again; I had enough of his tricks. All I need is a fresh start. I have always been thinking about a new beginning for some months now, but it seems like it isn't for me. But I will still try 'til I gain it. That was what I did from the very beginning; I started from nothing, and I never stopped until I am here, sitting in my house. I know, one day, I'll get the peace and rest that I wanted without my brother.

"Will it really happen?" I asked myself in silence.

I have been dreaming of peace, and a new start, but every time I that I would close my eyes, I could just picture Grace and Anthony in my mind. They have a wrongful relationship, and I never even did anything about it. How am I going to sleep at night knowing that my cousin, Garry, is being fooled by his own fiancé and Anthony? I don't know what will be my next step anymore. This is too much to handle.

I don't trust Anthony anymore, and the only hope that I have is Grace. But I cannot give my trust to her as well. She cried in front of me, so I would not tell Garry and his family. She promised me that she would leave Garry as soon as possible, but I know that she would not do it.

I don't want to see them anymore. I don't have anything to do with people who are hurting me. But how am I going to live thinking that I am supporting their shameless show, their unethical connection?

After thinking about all the brainless things, I poured another glass of wine, and checked my phone.

I received a text message with a home address, stated. "I finally reached her," I said to myself.

I phoned the number once again because of excitement, but this time, she never answered it. I left a voicemail and said, "Hi Diana. I am so glad to read your message. I will visit you as soon as possible. I will be very happy to see you."

For some unexplainable reason, I felt like I have to see her. I know that if I am going to meet her, there's a part of me that will surely be answered. Diana holds a part of my existence that can fulfil myself. After receiving the message, I immediately went to my room, and packed my belongings. I am ready to see her.

Chapter 16: She's Back

I am still here inside the four corners of this room. No memories tried to visit me, or made me remember. Everything is a mystery for me. Until now, my identity is unknown.

I've been reading the book for a long time now. The nurse promised me that reading would slowly help me, but it never happened. I am stuck in the middle of nowhere, without anyone to help me.

"I just don't know what to do", I said to myself.

While thinking about myself and what happened to me, I heard the creaking sound of the door, slowly opening. I looked immediately, and saw the doctor that I never liked. There is something wrong with him, and I can feel it. He is different from the rest of them, and I don't want him to be around.

"How are you?" the doctor asked.

"Why are my limbs still numb?" I asked.

The doctor looked at me with a sinister smile. He told me that I would be fine soon. He did not answer me.

"The nurse will give you four medicines, and after that, I have to do a further examination." the doctor said.

I am so eager to ask him a question, but it is too late. He already went out, and I was left behind, unanswered. Every person here in this place doesn't want to help, or maybe they couldn't.

After a couple of minutes, the nurse came and handed me over the medicines.

"Why do I have to drink this?" I asked the nurse in annoyance.

She turned around, and said, "If you want to get out of here, then you have to do whatever we say."

I swallowed the medicine, and never said anything. I trusted her for an unknown reason.

"Read as much as you can; it will help." The nurse said before leaving the room.

"Someone returns from deep down to start everyone's mourning."

After a long hour of travel from Durban to Cape Town, I finally reached Diana's place.

We decided to meet in a restaurant where Anthony and I first met. I saw her sitting and waiting for me. I called her name, and she gave me a beautiful smile. Diana looked different compared to how she was. It's been three decades ago since I last saw her, and there's no doubt that both of us changed, not only on how we think, but also on how we present ourselves.

"I wanted to see you for so long", I said.

We sat and started to talk about what happened to both of us for the last couple of years. Diana and I began in a very light conversation. We spoke about the jobs that we had experienced, and the family that we had. She was so happy telling her story about her kids and husband, and I also felt the same. I am glad to see her happy and smiling in the life that she has chosen.

She is running a big information technology company with her husband, and raising their two children who are both studying in a university.

Diana asked me about my life, and I didn't hesitate to tell her everything that I experienced in life. I told her the most strenuous, as well as the most successful job that I had, and she was genuinely happy about me advancing in ranks. I shared my married life that never lasted, and at the end of the conversation, we both had a good time.

"You know that you are my favourite cousin, right?" Diana spoke.

I laughed and asked why I am her favourite. Diana told me that on those days, I was the most blameless, but the most curious one. Hour passed by, and our conversation became deeper, causing the ambience to change. The happy start for both of us turned to a heavy emotion when I asked about her teenage life.

"I forgot, Kevin. I don't know what happened," she replied.

I never pushed her to tell me, nor demanded her for response. I let her keep it for the reason that it must be painful. I know that it was the worst to remember. After a long day spending with Diana, I decided to move, and told her that I need to go.

"Why can't you just stay with us, and spend time with my family," Diana said.

"Are you sure?" I asked.

She told me that I could sleep in their guest room. Her two kids were around, and it would be nice if I could spend some time with them. In the end, I agreed.

As we drive going to her house, I remember that Anthony is living close to where she is settling. My brother is staying in Camps Bay while she stays in Bantry

Bay. I thought about calling my brother, but I decided to talk to Diana first.

"Do you know that Anthony is living so near to you?"

I thought she never heard me, so I added, "Have you ever seen Anthony around here?"

She continued driving, set her eyes on the road, and said, "No, but he is always visiting me."

I was stunned, and didn't know what to say. We continued the journey, and just before I opened my mouth to ask her about Anthony, she told me that we are already in front of her house.

Diana's house is beautiful, just like the other houses. The properties in the area are expensive because of the demand, surroundings, and fantastic view. I am happy that she opened her home for me. I came inside and saw her children. Diana's daughter and son are both in their twenties. The interior of Diana's home is stunning. She got the fanciest entertainment area with a huge window, facing the ocean. The hallway is filled with trophies of achievements.

I saw her daughter's recognition certificate in martial arts and son's medals recognising his talent in the sports field and hunting. They are truly blessed with strength, as well as knowledge.

I spent my night with my nephew and niece, talking about school. I can see that their parents raised them very well. They are not just respectful and kind, but they are also bold and wise. I asked them where was their father, and Diana's son told me that their dad needed to go on a business trip to another country.

After an hour of sharing, we decided to go to bed, and Diana showed me the guest room. It was simple yet elegant. I am so glad that they welcomed and trusted me to stay in their house. I went to the shower, and cleaned myself. I cannot think any further; I had a long and exhausting day. All that I want is to sleep, and not to do anything anymore.

I reached the bed, and fell asleep.

■■

I have no idea what happened next. I never saw the time. It was already morning, and I didn't even realise it. I got up from the bed, took a bath and went outside the room.

"I made a breakfast for all of us", Diana said.

She called her children, and we all started to eat the food.

"We have to go now, mum", her son spoke, and they went away.

While at the table, Diana asked me how's my sleep, and I told her that I had a nice rest. We exchanged some words, and suddenly, the conversation stopped.

"Your brother doesn't need to visit me; he's always in my dreams, Kevin."

"Why?" I asked once again.

She looked at me, and gave me a forced smile. Diana told me that she didn't know why, and that she had no answer for that.

"Anthony is not wandering in my dreams, but we used to hang out before."

"And then one day, he started to use people, whoever he could, for his own, including me", I added.

Diana listened to me, and requested to tell me everything. And I did. I told her what Anthony had done not only to his brother, but also to his friend.

I started with how Anthony took loans using my name, made use of a trust document with his friend, ran away from all of his debts, and ruined a family just to get what he wanted. It could have been worse, and I am lucky enough to come out of it. I know that it was a devastating story to tell, but it will be far more unacceptable to forget.

The conversation between us became more personal. She just listened to me all this time. I shared my experience living and working with our Uncle Paul, telling her what torment I've been through all those years, and how I started to climb. Diana looked at me so that she could comfort me. She made me feel that way. I was delighted to release all the memories that I kept for so many years. Sometimes, we needed to let go of all the bad things so we can move forward. I never kept any pain within me. At that time, I took out everything inside for me to heal.

Diana responded and said, "It takes a lot of courage for you to do what you did."

I told her that she could say everything to me, and I would listen. At first, she was very hesitant, but she told me her whole story at the end.

Diana started talking about her teenage years. I could say that it wasn't normal for a person at young age to undergo those kinds of situation. I thought I had a rough life, until I heard Diana's side.

I was devastated hearing her story; I wanted to cry, but I couldn't. All these years, I thought that not involving in somebody else's life was the right thing to do, but I was wrong.

Diana shared her past situation inside the house of my Uncle and Auntie. She was abused and hurt by that time, which pushed her to move out of that place. My jaw almost dropped when she told me that our cousins, Willy and Garry, molested, and physically abused her, but their parents never did anything. Lorette shut her off because Diana caught our auntie cheating, and it seemed like Paul didn't do anything, or said something about it.

I am a living witness when my aunt Lorette cheated with the same good-looking man who talked unpleasant things about me, and I did nothing.

"If they have a child, or a small girl inside their house, I am sure that they are going to do the same thing as what they did to me." Diana said.

I cannot believe what I heard right now. Diana's words and confession reminded me of the two little girls, Nadia and Sunny. I was there when they were getting abused by their flesh and blood, but I never did anything about it again.

Diana was right. They did the same thing.

For so many years, I believed that ignorance is bliss, but not in the eyes of the victim.

There's a child who had been hurt, and there's a vile, immoral behaviour that was ongoing because I kept quiet.

I cannot say any more words. My past was nothing compared to what she experienced, and had been through. The regrets and guilt started to grow in me, and I hoped that I could still turn back the hands of time, but I couldn't.

"I should do something", I whispered to myself.

"Diana, I wish I was there", I said to her.

She stood up and put the plate in the sink. She turned around, and said, "You were there, Kevin, and I told you to be careful."

At this moment, I cannot understand what she was saying. I couldn't ask her for an explanation because there's no word coming out from my mouth. I was completely speechless. All that I did was to remember the times that Diana and I were together. I was trying my best to go back to the time when she told me to be careful, but I failed.

She looked straight into my eyes, told me to think properly, and said, "It was a festive season, Kevin, when I told you that I would not go back to that place again..."

"Unless you are dead", I finished her sentences, and all the memories of the past came back like a strike of lightning.

I remembered that time. It was Christmas Day, and I was only a twelve-year-old little boy. After spending holidays with us, Diana's last words were kept and buried as a mystery for me. And now, I have the answer. My whole life, I thought that I was a naive little Kevin, thinking that everything around me was a dream, but they weren't. She told me that she would never be back in our house, and that's the reason why I never saw her for so many years.

"The monster truly existed, Kevin, but it's not like what you think. I asked you to be careful, but you never did."

Chapter 17: Hide and Seek

I have been ringing Anthony's gate for so many times, but I got no response. I don't know how many properties he had, and where he is hiding.

I am in a complete disturbance. I never imagined myself, looking for my brother because of the pain that he had caused to someone. There is no explanation for what he did. Anthony needs to face his own nightmare. For so many years, I thought it was a dream, but it wasn't. I thought it was the monster lurking under the bed, but I was wrong.

The feeling of guilt is growing inside of me. I keep on asking myself why I never did anything to stop this. I am blaming myself for what happened. I decided to go back to Diana's house after trying to see Anthony. I handed over the key of her car that I borrowed, and sat outside to get some fresh air. I closed my eyes and said, "I'm so tired."

"So do I", Diana replied.

Time passed by, and there's no word that came out from the both of us. We ran out of thoughts, and all we did was to sit, thinking about the past that would never be right. I hope that I am smart enough to do something, but I'm not.

"Tell me. Can I still make these things right?" I asked.

Diana responded and said, "No, Kevin, they already happened."

My tears started to flow through my cheeks, and I felt the pain. I can no longer handle any of this. I know that I will break anytime soon. Diana went inside, and I am still sitting outside, waiting for nothing and mourning like a child.

I closed my eyes once again, and convinced myself that I have to see my brother. I grabbed my phone inside my pocket, and dialled Carl's number. He picked up the phone, and asked him what property did Anthony buy under the trust, and if he has access to any of it

.

Carl told me that one last property that was not yet sold because my brother never permitted it. He told me that he would try to get access to the area, and he gave me his word that he would phone me as soon as possible.

All that I need is to see Anthony, and I will do whatever it takes to get in touch with him. Half an hour passed by, and Carl phoned me as he promised. He gave me the address of the property, and informed me that it was a holiday home, and I just need to tell his name in the reception.

I drove for the second time, hoping that I would find my brother, or something that could help me to see him. After a long drive, I finally reached his holiday home. I did Carl's instruction, and they let me in.

It is surprisingly simple. The room is clean and there's nothing fancy, aside from the screen in the room. I checked every corner of the place, and found nothing; from bedrooms to the toilet, I found no Anthony. I sat for a while, and took a deep relaxing breath. I stared all over, and looked at his bookshelves. I was amazed by its retro style. I read the title of the books, and I could say that it was more of a thriller. The shelves slowly opened when I accidentally pushed the side of it. My jaw dropped to see another way at the back. Out of my curiosity, I walked inside, and saw another room that was hidden. I laughed inside of my head, saying, "This must be the place where Anthony has been hiding for so long."

However, there's no Anthony inside. It is just a room similar to an office. It is dark and very secluded. It has one chair and one table with a video player system on top. There are six tv monitors hanging on the wall, and cables that are connected to each other. To be honest, I have no idea what these things in front of me are, and from that moment, I started to ask myself what was the purpose of all of these. At first, I thought that it was meant for video footage security outside of the property. I clicked the button by luck, and the whole surveillance system opened up. I was shocked that it was connected to every part of the room; it could record things from the lounge to the bathroom.

I kept myself searching around, and spent hours for just a tiny room. At the end of my searching, I took one flash drive, lying inside a small cupboard, and put back everything exactly as how they were.

I left the property, and immediately phoned Carl to thank him for the favour that he had done.

"Carl, can I ask for one more thing?" I said to him.

"What is it?" He responded.

"Please don't tell anyone that I went to that place, even to Anthony."

Carl promised me that he is going to talk to the receptionists, and ask them to do the same thing. I am so glad that time. I know that Carl is a man of his own words. I spent the whole day looking for someone who didn't want to be seen. I stood in front of Diana, and she asked, "Where have you been?"

"Looking for the answer," I replied.

Diana's children were back from school, and my cousin made something to eat for them. They were so happy to be back home even though they were gone for only one day. While looking at them, I can't help but to question myself, "Is this the family that I wanted to ruin?"

I excused myself in front of everyone, and walked straight into the guest room. I lay down, and locked my eyes in the ceiling. I don't know what to do; I am frightened, and tired about my own life. Anthony never answered my phone call either. And for this time, I chose to send him a message.

"I already know what you did to Diana, and I know all the horrible things you have done."

While lying down in the bed, waiting for answer, I heard my phone ringing from an unknown number. My heart started to pound, and I answered the call without saying anything.

`'Do you know what I did to Diana, Kevin? Do you actually know everything?"

For some reasons, I cannot open my mouth. I cannot scream, or make a noise. The only words that came from me are, "You are the monster."

"Go ask your mother, why?" It was Anthony's voice speaking. He responded menacingly.

After Anthony's phone call, I tried to speak to mum, but she never picked up her phone. My brother confused, and messed my head once again.

The darkness swallowed the earth, and I walked into the four areas of this room, thinking about what I could do. Anthony's words made me think that, maybe, mum knows something, but I am doubtful. I was with mum all my life, and she would not allow any wrong acts of her own child. She taught us far better than this.

I went outside the room, and looked for my cousin. She was sitting in the lounge, watching a program. I sat beside her, and never said anything for a while. It was a complete silence.

After waiting, I opened up a conversation, like the usual. We talked and forgot about the horrible things that went through our minds. At the end of the conversation, I told Diana that I have to go back to Durban tomorrow morning. She asked me why I have to rush, and insisted that I have to stay for more days, but I really have to go.

"Cape Town to Durban is not a long flight, compared to an international flight. I'll definitely go to visit weekly, perhaps." I said to myself.

I got up, and walked away from Diana. I locked the guest room to rest, and decided to book a flight going back home to see mum immediately. I fell asleep shortly afterwards.

∎∎

The first thing that I did in the morning was packed my belongings. I had my breakfast together with Diana, as well as her kids. We left the house earlier; Diana offered that she would drive for me, instead of grabbing a taxi, and I agreed. After reaching the airport, I gave my cousin a tight hug, and said, "I'll make this situation better. I am sorry."

"It is over now. Please, don't." She responded.

Yet, in my head, I have to.

I took a flight for almost three hours going back home just to speak to mum. I want to know everything, and I want to clarify that my mother is not aware of what Anthony did to Diana. I immediately went to mum's house without rest. I knocked on the door, sat and confronted her.

"Did you know what happened to Anthony when we were young?"

She looked at me in confusion and said, "What do you mean? There were a lot of things that happened, Kevin."

"I can't even say it, mum. I can't even imagine it because that's the most disgusting act that I ever heard," I yelled.

"He said that you know it, and he said that he howled about it in front of you."

Mum set her eyes on the other side, and kept quiet. I realised that she really know something. Her confession made my head turn.

"All that I can remember is when he broke down in front of me because of Paul, intimidating him. He made your brother ill." Mum said.

"So, maybe, you're right. Maybe, it was outrageous." She added.

It wasn't clear, I asked mum what she meant, and she told me that she didn't know what happened between Anthony and Uncle Paul. The only thing that she was knowledgeable of was Anthony was so frightened, and cursed his own uncle to death. For that moment, I know that mum doesn't know anything about Diana and Anthony; her hands are undeniably clean with this.

But it was another story that opened up. It was a cold creep. My body started to shiver; it is a different nightmare that needs an answer.

"What did Paul do to Anthony?" I whispered.

There are a lot of questions playing in my mind. It seems like instead of getting answers, more uncertainties are coming. I started to know that Anthony was harassing Diana, and I ended up, questioning myself what happened between my brother and my uncle.

I paused for a while and think. I said not one word when mum suddenly spoke, and said, "That's what I can remember, son, and I don't know if it's bad or sickening."

"I never asked. I just hugged him, and cried with him that time." She added.

I couldn't make any conclusion. My brain stopped working, and I couldn't think any further. I was stuck asking myself what else do I have to know, and how many regrets do I have to feel for not doing anything.

I never did anything when I saw Sunny and Nadia, getting hurt inside Paul and auntie Lorette's home. I was there, but I didn't do anything. I never said a word when I saw my uncle and auntie, keeping themselves quiet while their son was hurting others long years ago. I am not different from them. I let my brother have an immoral relationship with Grace, and walked away without doing anything. Not for a moment, I understood what Diana told me three decades ago. I should've done something, but I was so dense to apprehend all of these deeds. The most unscrupulous act that I did was to think that all of these were just a bad dream. I thought that it was a long nightmare, but it wasn't. It was not a monster under the bed, and there's no disturbing creature, other than us. We were the beast of our own.

I understand that mum and I did the same thing. She never asked Anthony or Paul about what happened to both of them; it was the same thing that I did. I did nothing.

"Why did you never ask your son, or even Paul, mum?" I questioned.

"Because I was trying to save you, Kevin. I thought I have to do it.

Chapter 18: Uninvited Guest

I continuously read the book, and no memories came out. It was a complete darkness for me. I'm still here reading a novel that cannot help me in any way. Nobody deserves to go through this. The book seems not going to an end. It is a mystery, a story that is left unanswered.

This room is filled with loneliness. I feel like many people had been here, and never made it. The atmosphere is different: there's no light, and the beautiful view is on the other side. I can hear the screams of humans like they are burning inside the chamber of fire, and the worms are eating their flesh. No happiness in this place, nor air to breathe. It's just a complete anguish.

I turned my head, looked at them through the window, and said to myself, "I wish that I could go, and walk there."

The doctor came to my room and spoke, "Let's hope that you can enjoy the other side."

He picked up the book, looked at it very sternly, and handed it over to me.

"Finish it." He said.

"The past holds our tomorrow, and our tomorrow will write our fate."

It is another month of this terrible year for me. I have to change the calendar hanging on my wall; I tore the month of June, and the 2nd of July caught my attention. It was circled in red. I forgot what is it all about, honestly. I thought that, maybe, it was an important meeting, and I looked at my phone to check.

It is my cousin and Grace's wedding. I have no idea if they continued their relationship. I remember that my cousins, Mervin and Addie, together with their parents, came here from Australia to attend the family celebration. I was advised that Garry will be tying the knot so soon.

I never got shocked when Grace would still be marrying Garry, while having a secret relationship with my brother. Like what most people say, birds of the same feathers flock together. From that moment, I was already aware of why I wasn't invited; it was because I knew something more than other people.

Who would ever expect that every one of us has a huge dark secret inside? To keep the sanity of a man, carrying a closed book, is more complicated than carrying the world.

I went to the kitchen, made myself a coffee and sat. I am now thinking about what am I going to do for the day. I phoned Diana, and we talked about her day. We already had a quite long conversation when I asked her if she is not busy this week; luckily, she's not.

"Do you want to see them again?" I said

"I am not sure," Diana replied.

I told her that Garry's wedding would be this week, and everyone would be there. I insisted, just for her to come, and she agreed at the end. We are the uninvited guests, gate crashers, as they said. She made me aware that the place is still clear to her memory, and that I don't need to send her the address of our relatives. I was happy at that moment.

Our story was endless; we talked longer than before, and enjoyed the phone call from two different sides.

"I think, we can write a masterpiece out of your story." She chuckled.

"Can we actually do that? I'll tell you everything, and you'll write them down for me." I responded.

Diana smiled at me and said; "Of course, I will."

We dropped the phone call, and did separate things.

▪▪

Days passed by, and I travelled a day before the wedding. Diana told me that we have to meet for the reason that she booked separate rooms for her and me in Melrose North, Johannesburg. I am glad that she came; I feel like every one of us needs to face the fear that we once felt. I believe that we have to embrace the past for us to move on. No one must live in misery. Someone has to pay.

I reached the place, and saw Diana, waiting for me in front of the well-structured hotel that she chose for us. She gave me a smile- a smile that is way brighter than what I was used to.

"Are you ready?" I asked.

"I have to, I guess." Diana said.

After the night of waiting, the sun finally rose. I had a bath, used one of the finest clothes that I brought, and waited for Diana to have breakfast with me in the restaurant that I reserved for the two of us. Not so long when she walked towards me, and sat by the table.

Diana is wearing a long black gown, which represents hatred. Her lips are red that symbolises anger, and her sinister smile means revenge. However, they are just my own interpretations. I don't know what is playing inside her mind, and I feel like I am not in control of that.

We enjoyed the food, and decided to go to the closest mall in the area. She requested me to wait for her as she would buy a gift for them, and I willingly did it. I waited for a couple of minutes, and Diana finally got what she wanted. I started the car, and drove going to my relatives' place. The more that we get closer to the place, the farther that it gets for me. It was a long and exhausting journey for me.

"We're finally here." Diana said.

Diana and I jumped off the car, and rang the bell of the property. Uncle Paul opened the door for us. He gave me a smile, but it slowly faded when he saw the familiar face of a woman.

"Who invited you here?" Uncle Paul asked Diana.

"Am I not a family?" She responded.

We went inside the house, and saw everyone. Our extended family came, and gave us a hug. Everyone's eyes were full of loathing, asking themselves why Diana and I were there. We were not welcome. But all of us are actors; we pretended that everyone seemed to be going well, but we were not. Grace didn't want to see me. I knew what she did, and it made her worry. My auntie and my uncle, together with my cousins, were intimidated by Diana's presence. People at this celebration did something to each one of us.

For some reasons, I liked seeing the annoyance and the trembling on them. It was not enough for what they did, but it was a good start. The party started, and it was a pretended happiness. Some got drunk, some lost control, and some kept their mind out of track; I don't know which one I am.

While everyone was busy outside the main house, I went inside my uncle's office that once became my room. The paint is entirely different from what I could remember. The ceiling is new, and the appliances are shining. I looked around for no stable reason, thinking that I might find something pertaining to Anthony and Paul.

"What are you doing here?" Paul said.

I turned around, and said;

"I know what all of you did, not only to Diana, but also to Anthony and to this home."

He just smiled, unbothered, and asked me to tell every single thing that I know. So, I did. I told him that I know the horrible things that he and his son did to Diana. I never stopped myself from telling my uncle that I saw him doing nothing when Garry was hurting and interfering his own sister, Sunny, because she is another man's child.

"You know that Lorette was cheating on you, with your friend, but you did nothing. Instead, you let the poor child suffer. I was there," I added.

"And what did you do Kevin?" He asked.

I never stopped from that. I spilled things that could ruin someone else's life, and this time, I don't feel any remorse.

"For so many years of not doing anything, this is the time that I have to do something." I silently said.

"You don't know who you really are, Kevin. I am older than you. I know more things." He answered.

My uncle's words spun my head around. I don't know what he meant, but I told myself that I would not allow him to play with me again. I learnt my lesson. People manipulated us for their own benefits. They were turning things around for someone to look guilty for the things that they made up. That's how evil human works.

"No, uncle, I know more. I even know what you did to Anthony." I said.

I don't really know what Uncle Paul did to Anthony; I'm just hoping that he'll tell me more about it.

However, his next statement made me feel sick. My guts turned upside down. I could not imagine what he was saying.

"You remember what you did?" He continued.

I cannot look at him any longer. His story is unbelievable and untrue. We can no longer listen to each other. No one is telling the truth. All are for one's self.

"Did you even realise how you get away with rape, Kevin?" Paul said.

"It was a mistake. I never abused anyone. I am not like you." I responded.

He just laughed at me, telling me that he would not believe what I would say. Paul looked at me in the same way that he looked at himself, and I didn't like it.

"I am the one who set you free from jail," uncle Paul said.

He was continuously messing my mind by telling me lies. I decided to walk away from him, and not disturb myself by thinking that there's some actuality on his tale.

"You know what I did to your brother?" Paul asked.

I looked back and waited for him to talk, but instead of telling me the reality, he carried on with his story beyond belief—an inconceivable myth.

"I made Anthony quiet for the things that you did when you were young. You should thank me." He added.

The next time that I remember was I went out, and got some drinks for myself. My relatives never changed; they still have inexpensive drinks. I took some of it, and slowly felt the toxins in my body. I sensed that I was out of control.

I walked into the venue, and saw Willy alone, sitting by the table. I whispered to him and said, "I know what you did to Diana and your daughter Nadia many years ago, Willy. I know everything."

I did the same thing to Garry. I talked to him and said, "Do you remember what you had done to your sister, Sunny, and our cousin Diana? Look back, Garry." And I walked away.

I saw Grace, stepping towards Garry's table. I smiled at her and asked, "Is my brother Anthony not invited?"

She never answered me, and ignored my question. There's a part of me enjoying what I was doing. I could see the fear in their eyes; my words made their blood run cold, and all of their actions started to change. There's a time when a secret is powerful enough to hold someone responsible for what they did.

I sat with Diana, and we were talking nicely to each other. She told me that she was just talking to other guests, and was very happy that she was no longer hiding anymore. I am very happy for her, honestly. I couldn't agree more when she told me that it was better to face our nightmares, than live in fear for something that we never did.

I am happy to see her, embracing the fact that it is not her fault why our cousin Garry and Willy molested her. Not only them, but also my brother. I can breathe nicely seeing her not blaming herself why our auntie and uncle never did anything when she was hurt. I cannot hide my gladness witnessing all of them in fear, and paying for what they have done.

"Promise me that you'll help to write my life journal," I told her.

She beamed with pleasure, and said, "We will surely do it, Kevin."

We laughed together about what we did today. Both of us visited the people who hurt us, and it was like a bone that finally came out of our throat after staying there for so long. Diana and I can now breathe freely.

She asked me to go back to the hotel because I was consuming much more alcohol than before. Just when Diana helped me stand, we heard the long extensive scream of a woman asking for help. Every guest stood up, and got shocked at what they heard. Every one of us was stunned by what we saw. Their eyes were full of fear when they found a dead body.

"What have we done in this place?" I asked myself.

Chapter 19: Blood

"Let's see what's inside," I said to myself while inserting the flash drive into my computer.

I looked through the file, and was shocked at what I saw.

"How many horrible things did my brother do?" I asked myself in silence.

I searched more closely, and saw all disturbing videos that were saved in the storage. Too many different, rich, and powerful personalities were having intercourse, not with only one but many people. Hundreds of tapes were taken to Anthony's property.

I never had reasons why I took the flash drive from that place. I was just looking for him. I took something that contains files of different people, something that was not just an ordinary possession; it was something different.

"Why would he do that?" I questioned the air once again in disbelief.

As I was continuously looking through the files, I remember familiar faces that were in the videos. I recognised Anthony's two friends that I met and drank with when I first reconciled with him. Yet, I still couldn't understand why he did all these kinds of things. Not only videos were there, but also documents of his wealth and properties. I realised from this moment that I would have a huge difficulty.

I cannot understand what is going on. I don't know what's his motif for doing this kind of work. I looked at him as a greedy and immoral man, but, is there something that I could see about him more than this? It's unbelievable for a man, that seemed to have everything, to behave this way. Anthony was raised with love and attention. He climbed early in his life that most people couldn't do, and it made me wonder why he ended up like this. Is it nurture, or nature? I don't know.

The last file that was kept made my whole body fall to the ground; it was about me. The file was full of documents about Anthony's shares on my wealth, my medical records containing my mental health which were untrue, and my last will with my forged signature. Everything that I have would go to his hands once I die, or once he proves that I'm mentally incapable of handling my own life. This was more than greed. This was the hunger for every single thing. Anthony is living in riches beyond the dream of an avarice.

I never signed any document, and I couldn't remember when all of this happened. It was not me, and I am sure about it. The files were all spurious claims about my possessions.

"Did he drugged me to sign all of this?" asking myself for hundred times.

What's worse than seeing this kind of life. I witnessed tapes of different known people who have respectable positions and power having intimate affairs with many women, hundreds of documents giving Anthony the ability to handle somebody else's business and money, and, the downfall for me was to see myself in it. I would also be a victim.

While staring at my computer monitor, I gradually understood why he needed to do this. I remember the numerous screen monitors hanging on the wall of his secret room, and the cameras connected in every part of the property that, I once thought, were for security purposes, but they weren't. They were traps for his victims. For as long as he has the power to hold them on their neck, he would continue doing it.

He uses the videos to threaten them, and in exchange, he'd gain power or position. That's how psychotic, but smart, my brother is. Anthony uses all of these for his benefit.

I felt mad, I wanted to hurt him so badly, but I couldn't. He was the monster hiding under my bed, but I never looked at it. I fed the beast, and now it is eating me alive, taking all the things that I built for life. How are ordinary people supposed to react to this situation? My hands were looking for his blood, and I couldn't stop it. I just wanted to see him right away.

My flesh and blood meant to destroy me. He was the one who planned to use my buses to transport drugs from places to places. It was on his file; it was saved on a tiny storage that is now in my hand. He just didn't want to ruin me; he wanted me dead.

I sent messages to Anthony, saying, "I think I got the things that you want. Would you like to have it?"

Not so long when I heard my phone rang; it was an unknown number, but my instinct said that it was him.

I answered the phone call and said, "Meet me, and I'll give it back to you."

The line was cut off, and I heard no voice from the other side. I was right. It was him, looking for his crucial possession.

I went to my bed in agony. I breathed heavily, and looked through the open space. My room is in complete darkness. I can feel that my life has started to go down. I stopped making investments for a long time. There was a time when I even forgot to check my businesses. I think I mislaid my life. While lying in my bed, I sensed an unusual feeling rushing into my skin. I screamed aloud when I saw worms coming out under my bed. I could feel the heat inside my room, and there's no air to breathe in. I screamed so many times, but I lost.

Then, I woke up.

It was a nightmare, just like what I used to have. I am still stuck to the young Kevin who was frightened of his dreams. I opened my eyes; I was bathing with my sweat. My bed is soaked, and no one can help me to move. The room is already swallowed with light. I never felt that the night passed. It was quick for me. My body is still tired; however, the day needs to start.

I spent a couple of minutes lying down without moving. It was not because I didn't want to, but I simply couldn't. But in the end, I did.

I took my time, and washed my body. I dressed up and pushed myself to do something good for this day. I phoned my assistant, and asked how things are going with my investments, properties, and transportation company. She told me that everything is still working well, but my businesses will need me sooner or later. I need to start picking up myself soon. I went to work and tried to act like a normal human being, handling myself the best possible I can.

■■■

The day started to fall, and I decided to go to eat in a restaurant. I drove and chose one of the finest food places in my area. The server guided me to my table, and gave me their special menu. I chose steak, and a bottle of red wine for the night. As I was waiting, there's an unfamiliar man who walked towards me, and asked, "Hey, Kevin, do you remember me?"

"No, I am sorry," I answered.

He sat in front of me, insisting his name. I do not want him to be close to me, neither to know who he is. He told me that we should hang out together with the other boys before. However, I couldn't remember him. I just smiled and said, "It sounds like a gang, is it?"

"Well, we used to call ourselves like one", the man responded.

Now, I can slowly remember. We were in our metric class, and I was involved in a company of young and naïve individuals- the gang who was doing stupid things when we were teenagers. Well, I guess we were pretty dumb that time.

He kept on talking to me, and laughed so loud while remembering our story way back in high school. He reminded me of how I mistakenly read one line in William Shakespeare's book. What made me irritated was he couldn't fully remember what exactly happened, but this man in front of me kept on pushing memories that I didn't want to remember or even think about. He wanted to show how stupid I was. It made me feel that he was pushing me to the edge of my patience.

But instead of acting up, I remained calm. I tried to handle myself for the whole day, and I would not let anyone ruin it. However, the man continued.

He told me that they would swap my food for somebody else's lunch because my mum would always make the best food. I was very young at that time, and every day, I asked myself why mum was only giving me fried egg and rice. I thought that it's the only thing that she could provide, but my so-called friends took all those things away. I knew that mum did her best to feed me, but I never expected someone to steal my mum's hard-earned effort.

It wasn't about the food that they stole, it was about my mum, thinking that I was eating the good meal that she provided for me. From that moment, I was imagining punching his face while he was loudly laughing. I could feel the heat on my face; I could see the veins showing on my skin, and my fist was tightly closed. I was ready to hurt him in front of many people, but I never did it. I forcedly laughed, and politely asked him if he could leave the table because my order would come.

"By the way, what is your name again?" I asked.

"Jay-r. Nice seeing you again." He responded.

My whole body got angry; I never touched the food, and I was just patiently waiting for Jay-r to finish his time. After he ate, and used the comfort room, I followed him in a way that he would not see me. I was behind him in the dark.

He reached the parking lot where it seemed that there was no camera, no people. I grabbed his neck, folded my arms on it, and dragged him facing the floor so he couldn't see me. I hit and kicked his back so many times that I couldn't count. I left him in the gloom with his fatal condition. I left the place while he was crying in pain; I ran into my car and immediately started it. I normally drove as nothing happened.

I phoned Anthony, and gave him the address where we needed to meet. I was aggrieved by everyone else. My hand started to seek revenge. All I was thinking about was vengeance. Nothing else. I reached the place where I asked Anthony to come; it was partially dark. It was our playing area in the park many decades ago, but now, it was abandoned.

He looked at me very angrily, asking for his flash drive. We argued about all the things that he did to me, and to everyone else. Anthony just told me that it wasn't my business, and it made my blood boil.

"How about you molesting Diana, and the secret between you and Uncle Paul? My properties that you badly wanted? Are those matters not my business?" I screamed in despair.

Anthony chuckled, and kept on saying that it was all my fault. I never understood it. He was blaming me for all of the downfalls that he experienced in his life. I might be in rage towards him, but his wrath was incomparable.

"You did not do anything, Kevin. You are the one who put me here." Anthony said.

He admitted molesting Diana, and made me pay for the things that I did, but I just couldn't remember what happened. I was too young at that time, and all my memories were blocked.

I questioned Anthony and said, "What have I done to you for you to put me on this? I never did anything."

"You knew that our father died not because of me, but you kept quiet for your own sake," Anthony said.

"Paul did it, but insisted that I killed dad, and you never said anything," He added.

■■■

Memories were coming back, making my mind spin. My head started to ache, and when I woke up, there was no Anthony. I am sitting in a hospital senseless. However, the memories of my past are now apparent to me.

"This is my story; this book is me," I said to myself.

Chapter 20: Revelation

"Are you awake?" asked the doctor.

I was in the midst of surprise when the doctor came in. I couldn't remember how many times did he check on me, but this moment is different. My memory slowly comes into existence. It feels like my feet are trudging in the sand, and they leave footprints beyond. Prints of our past that were once blown by the wind; nothing was left behind. However, the memories remain; our minds might forget, but our hearts will always remember- things that we have done, either good or bad, evil or righteous.

"How's the book? Is it good?" The doctor asked once again.

I never answered him. I looked into the other side, and all the things that happened in the past came back. I thought I would have freedom by remembering all of these, but I'm wrong. It is a true nightmare that not all humans could stand.

I suddenly felt a sharp pain running into my head. I felt like I fell to the ground. The worst part was I was losing my sanity. I saw blood trickling and spilling all over from my broken skull. However, it was a figment of imagination. It wasn't true. I was delusional. I saw my dad falling from the fourth level of Paul's newspaper factory. His head hit the floor, and the blood splashed on me. The lifeblood splattered all over, including his broken bones. And I, sensed the pain.

I saw Anthony above screaming for our father, and crying, but he was not alone; there was someone behind him. I couldn't figure it out. It wasn't clear, but now I understand.

It was Paul who killed my father, and at the same time, he blamed Anthony for it. It was not my brother's crime, but he paid. He lost his mind because of what our uncle did. Paul created a monster that ruined every one of us. He turned Anthony into a beast that was ready to eat anyone. He held my brother's neck, and harassed him, but I never did anything. I never spoke, nor stood for Anthony.

"You have a visitor, Kevin," the doctor said.

He finally called me by my real name after I read the book of my life. This doctor is not here to cure me, but he is around to show me something, and I don't know what it is. Besides, I am still paralysed—no power to stand and incapable of seeing what is happening on the other side. Every part of me wants to leave this place, but something is not right.

My heart started to pound, and it was beating faster than before. I was waiting for whose face would show, and I was in immense shock when I saw Anthony's face. He looked at me without repentance.

"You put me here," I said to Anthony.

He bent his knee and looked straight in my eyes, and said, "You put yourself here for doing nothing."

I don't know what I am going to answer. He is right; I was too fool not to understand things. I was tongue-tied to speak up, and say something. I did nothing from the very beginning, thinking that it was the right thing to do. I let different evils to continue their wickedness in life, and that's the biggest sin that I did.

"You are just like our mother."

I responded to him and said, "Mum never knew what happened, and if she did, she would help you."

Anthony just laughed, with his tears almost coming out from the lid of his eyes, and said, "You are right. She didn't know what happened to me because she never asked. Mum was too busy protecting the wrong person."

The moment that I spoke to mum, one night, just quickly came into my head. I remember when she told me that she was trying to protect me and she had to do it.

It is clear, just like the tears running from my eyes. Uncle Paul told mum that I was the one who pushed dad because of my recklessness, and she didn't try to ask anything about it. She was scared to lose me after losing her husband. But if she just put a question, she would understand what truly happened, and who started it.

Paul has compulsive sexual behaviour that drove him to kill dad, and sexually assaulted Anthony.

My brother is right. It was because of me. I just watched, and did nothing.

"This is enough, Anthony. I want to go back home." I spoke.

"Close your eyes, Kevin, and remember all the things that you did. Close them now." Anthony said.

I closed my eyes and tried to think about all the unrighteousness that I did. I remembered chasing money, partying night and day, forgetting about my family, and hanging out with the wrong people. But all of these were nothing compared to what I chose in life. I kept quiet and closed my eyes when there were innocent children getting abused by the wicked ones. What made me different from them is ultimately nothing. I am just like them that live on this earth without purpose, but to hurt others.

I opened my eyes when I heard Anthony talking, "You might forget what happened to Paul and me. Think again, search and remember."

I heard voices and murmurs all over. My illusion started, and I saw people crying everywhere. I heard a sharp and ear breaking howl of a woman, asking for help. Her eyes were full of horror and fear. She saw a lifeless body of a man; she found Paul's body.

I woke up from my illusion, and I ran out of air. I couldn't breathe properly, and there are too much questions in my head.

"What happened?" I asked myself.

Anthony came to me closely, whispered into my ears, and said, "That's right, Kevin. Ask yourself what happened."

I cannot handle my mind. I am losing control of myself. I wanted to wake up from my nightmare, but I couldn't. It seems like I am facing an impossible reality. Horrible episodes were continuously coming, and I had no idea what was real and what was not. I saw Anthony covered with blood and not breathing, but now, he was standing in front of me. I knew that they were using this to harm me, and that there's no reality on this.

"You are not dead, Anthony. You are standing here alive." I screamed.

"You are a monster of your own, Kevin. Continue, because there's a story that you still need to remember." He responded.

I started to feel the heat inside the room. It was becoming hotter and more as the seconds went by. What happened next took my breath away.

The room started to decay. The spotless white room was now covered by dark matters. I was horrified; I didn't know what to do. I wanted to scream, but I couldn't; there was no air to breathe, and there were no words to speak. The neat bed turned into a rough stone, and the whole place became my cell. It was no longer a hospital. It was a filthy, sticky prison cell. I was inside the chamber of death, secluded with bars on the pit.

The intense heat caused me extreme thirst, and there's not one drop of water in this place. My mind was wondering how people could stay alive with this kind of hotness. I could see the world, and feel the absence of light. The agony was all over in this dark abyss. I had no strength in my body, the constant pain and struggle were my reality, and the severe dryness of my throat continued. I was in extreme desire for a single drop of fluid.

If it was a hallucination, I just wanted all of these to be done. If it's only a nightmare, I would never get back to sleep. I badly wanted to wake up, but I was in consciousness, begging for air and water in the abode of the dead. Aside from this cell not having air to breathe, there was a disgusting smell on each side of the chamber that no could handle. The scent was dreadful that would force everyone not to inhale. It was more like sulphur, and could quickly kill anyone who was fool enough to catch the wind.

I know that I am dying, but this is only a bad night of dreams. It seems like I am not going to change. I'm still keeping the young and naive Kevin inside of me. The young boy who's still afraid of his dream. I helped myself and tried to wake up. The sound of the people, crying, is still playing in my head. It took a second for me to look and see this place once again.

I am in a different world. It took me back to where it almost ended. I was at Garry's wedding, and everyone was happy, laughing and busy making memories when our uncle Paul was found lifeless. The giggles turned into wailing, the smiles turned into sadness, and every one of us were left unanswered.

There was no blood, but only a dead body.

In the blink of an eye, everything changed. I witnessed a legion of demons scattered inside, and the enormous animal chained into the wall, burning in fire. I wanted to throw up as I saw the appearance of the reptile, creeping towards me with open wounds, and the worms were going in and out; however, there was nothing left on me.

Everything started to become dark and foggy. I couldn't take this anymore; it was exceedingly real. My brother turned into a bloody human, and his body was found where we last saw each other. I didn't know what happened between him and me, but he was dead. Paul is dead; No pulse, no soul, and no life to breathe. I was just looking at him showering with his blood in an abandoned place where we met. I just wanted to talk to him about all of the things that he did, and now, I don't know what happened. It's either I forgot, or I utterly didn't want to remember.

I am screaming for help, but no one can hear me. It is not a nightmare; I guess I am in hell.

The evils were cursing and hating God because of their rebelliousness and pride. They wanted to be God of their own, and rule amongst men. Evil ones wanted the earth, and the suffering of humans was a blissful thing for them. This place is for the agony of death, and their torture of a lifetime.

Anthony spoke to me once again, and said, "It is not you, Kevin. You never did this."

"You were dead, and I saw you dead," I said to Anthony.

"I am." He responded.

Now is the time to pay. It is the result of everything. I am right inside the darkness with the monster that I am always dreaming of when I was young. This is no longer a nightmare but my fate. This is how my life was written by myself, and I think I am the one who chooses this way. That's how I make my bed in hell.

People are burning and screaming loud, asking for water and help. Their skin and flesh are hanging on their bones, and the maggots are crawling over them. The giants, with monstrosity behaviour and look, are throwing all the helpless people into the lake of fire. Everyone is crying because of pain, but the demons hear nothing. They will do the same thing over and over again. There is no peace here, only fear and terror.

My turn finally came. The monster with long claws, sharp teeth and treacly skin dragged me from my rough stone bed and threw me. I heard my bones broke apart inside, and the pain was throbbing.

All I can do is cry and ask for help.

I questioned myself, and said, "Why am I here? What happened to me?"

The doctor changed his appearance. I knew that there was something wrong with him, and I was right. From a fine and excellent man, he turned into a beast. He answered my question and said, "Nothing. It happened because you did nothing."

The monsters slowly walked towards me and readied themselves to rip off my flesh into pieces. I calmly closed my eyes, hoping that I would wake up, but I only saw Diana sitting beside me, smiling. I was asking myself why she's in this kind of place. Maybe it was another illusion, but she talked to me. I heard her voice calling my name and saying something.

"I did it, Kevin; I did it to them and you."

I saw her with Paul, and I just looked at her as if nothing happened. She was there beside Anthony's lifeless body. I was the living witness to what happened, but I kept quiet. Diana killed Uncle Paul and Anthony for revenge.

"I killed them and you because I wanted to bury everything for the rest of my life." She added.

"And I did not say a single thing", I responded.

In a short glimpse, I am back at hell, a chamber of dead people who are full of anguish and despair, a long way of torment and an incessant desolation.

I now understand and remember every single thing. My brother and my uncle are dead because I just looked and kept quiet. Further to this, it isn't because of Diana, who killed me, that brought me here in hell. I am in here because of doing nothing. This is the payment for what I did, perhaps.

The monster dragged me, and almost tore me apart. They were prepared to throw me away into the prodigious lake of fire, and they did. I felt my skin and flesh falling off my bone, the worms are just all over me, and then someone pulled me from the dead.

■■■

"Wake Up. Please wake up." Someone is talking beside me. I am back in my spotless bed, and there are no dark matter in the clean white wall.

I am back where the hell doesn't exist.

"Where am I, and who are you?" I asked.

"You are in the hospital, and I am your nurse, Foi, remember? You were dreaming, I guess," she responded.

"A bad dream within a dream, I think," I responded.

"The only thing necessary for the triumph of evil is for good men to do nothing."

- Edmund Burke.

About the Author

Keegan Naidoo is one of the well-praised wealth managers in one of the biggest banks in South Africa way back in 2014, investing close to billion Rands of people's money. However, he was diagnosed with anxiety and severe depression that affected his relationship with other people. He was battling with his physical disability since that same year, making it difficult for him to move for eight years now.

Keegan wrote his first fictional story, amongst many, before his disability occurred, and never had a chance to publish it because of his physical and mental situation. But now, his family and team helped him make this happen.

He is out of work due to his mental and physical disability, and still under treatment.

Dear Reader

First of all, I just wanted to say that you are looking lovely today. Your smile can be compared to dazzling stars on a beautiful night. Your eyes are brighter than the sun; they are full of love, full of hope, and full of happiness.

Happiness- that's what matters the most. Most of us are chasing a life that we even forgot about ourselves because we are too caught up of the things on earth. Sometimes, all that we need to do is to sit back and ask ourselves: Am I happy? Or is this making me truly happy?

I am sure that you don't know me, but here I am, introducing myself. I am Keegan Naidoo. For 38 years in this world, I feel like I've never been so joyful in life for the reason that I am chasing the wrong things. Just like other people, I have also been through a lot. I was diagnosed with severe depression and, in this current time, I am battling with my physical disability.

Life is hard, not only to me but also to you. But take time and look at yourself now. Isn't it that you can stand, you can laugh and you are breathing? You know why? Because you are strong enough. It means that you can be happy whenever you want, so go for it!

I remember the days when I spent most of my time working at the wrong companies, and doing naive things. I thought that's what happiness meant, but I am wrong. It wasn't and it will never be.

I walked with people doing erroneous things, and I never did anything or even say something. They are my family, they are my friends, and whatever unrighteous deed that they are doing, for me, it is fine. That's what kind of man I was back then. I once thought that it was the right thing to do because it made me laugh, it made me happy for a moment- just for a very short moment. However, I forgot that by doing nothing, while seeing people behaving iniquitous in front of me, I am making my bed in hell, a place where there's no true joy, a place filled with suffering, and a place covered by darkness.

One day, you will understand what my book is about. It is about life. A life where there is no bliss because the character never had the voice to stand up, and say, "It is not how it is supposed to be"

We cannot condone or support somebody else's sin; the creator is watching us above. He knows everything about us.

I want you to know that happiness doesn't come with the wrong reason; happiness is when you know what is right, and you stand up for it. I wish that you'll find happiness for the right and long-lasting ground, because you deserve it.

By writing this book, I found myself. I found my joy.

I will pray for you that tomorrow, you'll get up, and finally find joy by doing what is right, and only right.

Lots of love,
Keegs